SLEEP WELL!

by
Kenneth Ireland

ℛℛ

RAVETTE PUBLISHING

First published by Ravette Publishing 2001

Printed and bound in Great Britain
for Ravette Publishing Limited,
Unit 3, Tristar Centre,
Star Road, Partridge Green,
West Sussex RH13 8RA
by Cox & Wyman Ltd, Reading, Berkshire

ISBN: 1 84161 030 5

CONTENTS

SLEEP WELL

"At half-term," said Alan, "we could go camping – just the two of us."

"Camping? That early in the year? You're joking!" replied Danny. "It's far too cold. The tent will probably get covered in snow!"

"Youth hostelling, then," suggested Alan. "Hardly anybody else will be around, so we'll probably have the place to ourselves. If we can find a hostel open, of course."

That sounded better. They looked at the Youth Hostels Handbook and then at a map.

"It won't cost much," enthused Alan. "I'm a member, and you could join easily. Look at the map. If we caught a bus to there and then walked about ten miles, we could reach the first hostel in plenty of time."

"Trudging through the snow?" put in Danny, still doubtful.

"Maybe," replied Alan, "but that won't matter, not with decent boots on. All we'd need in our packs would be sleeping bags, a change of clothes in case we get wet and a few odds and ends."

Alan's parents were the sort who would let him do anything. Danny's parents, on the other hand, were not so easy-going, and so it came as a great surprise to him that they were happy to let him go with Alan.

"It should be perfectly safe for the two of you," said his mother. "As long as you don't do anything stupid like accepting a lift from anybody."

"Of course not," said Danny.

It turned out they had both been youth hostellers themselves once.

"Years ago, of course," said his father. "We had some good times in youth hostels. You'll have to do the chores, of course."

"What are they?"

"Peel the spuds, do the washing-up, clean out the dormitories, that sort of thing. That's what we had to do. It's how they keep the prices low. That's how it used to be, anyway."

"It still is," confirmed Alan. "But that's no big deal."

"So where are you thinking of going?"

They showed them the map.

6

"We've checked and these will be open. First night there, second night there, and the third night ..." Alan plonked his finger firmly on the spot. "There, St Edmund's Castle!"

"We fancy staying a night in a castle, even if it is only a little one," explained Danny.

"You'd better write and book these places, then," said his father agreeably. So they did.

*   *   *   *   *

They could see some snow high up on the hills as they walked along the valleys, but the weather wasn't bad at all. It was quite warm, but a bit wet underfoot here and there.

There were not many other backpackers at the first two hostels at which they stayed. Danny almost enjoyed doing his chores – until the novelty wore off!

They had an evening meal and breakfast in each of the hostels. For lunch, they bought sandwiches and an apple from the warden which lasted them through the day.

"Now for the really interesting place," said Alan, as they set off on their final hike to their third night's stay.

As a castle, St. Edmund's was disappointing. It was rather small with no battlements and just one tower. It stood quite close to the road in the village, opposite a church. The handbook said that a king had once used it as a hunting lodge. Still, it was a genuine castle that dated back to Norman times.

When they signed in, Alan and Danny were delighted to find that they were the only ones staying there. So they would have the whole castle to themselves – apart from the warden, a sour-faced, middle-aged woman.

"Since you two are the only ones here," she snapped, "lights-out will be early, half-ten at the latest. I don't want to hear any noise after that and no messing about, either. I'm putting you in a little room at the top of the castle. You should enjoy it up there!"

The woman went on to say that it was Danny's job to help prepare supper in the kitchen. They both had to help with the washing-up afterwards and, in the morning, Alan's task was to clean and tidy their bedroom.

"That'll be all right," said Alan.

"I know it will," replied the warden, sternly.

They found the room at the top of the stairs and along a short corridor. It wasn't bad, just a bit bare and small. There were two bunk beds in it. The lavatory and washroom were just along the corridor.

Next to their room was another door.

They opened it out of curiosity and peered inside. It was very similar to theirs, but a little larger, and the only other room on their landing.

It was fascinating, almost spooky, to wander about the castle after they'd done the washing-up that evening. The warden didn't seem to mind. After all, why should she? They weren't interfering with anyone else.

They found their way to the tower and discovered just one small room with an ancient fireplace in one corner. This room was totally empty. A little plaque over the doorway stated that Mary Queen of Scots had once spent a night there.

"Not a very big room for a queen to stay in," commented Alan.

"I expect she was a prisoner at the time," said Danny, "being taken somewhere else." He didn't know much about history, but he did remember something like that had happened to Mary Queen of Scots.

"This isn't a bad place at all, is it?" he commented.

"It would be better with a bit more light," grunted Alan.

The warden seemed to be economising on electricity. The only lighting along the corridors consisted of dim bulbs fitted into wall brackets. The only way they could see anything in this room was when the moonlight came in through one of the narrow windows. Alan would have been happier waiting until morning to look around, but he wasn't going to tell Danny that.

There was a call up the stairs.

"Boys! The lights will be out in five minutes!" shouted the warden.

"Quick ... pyjamas and a wash," said Alan. They hadn't realised it was so close to lights-out.

They had just returned to their room and were getting into their bunks when the dormitory light went out abruptly.

"She doesn't mess about, does she?" grumbled Danny.

"We've got a torch," Alan reminded him, switching it on. He shone it at the light bulb.

"It's burned out," he said, "and gone black. She didn't switch it off from somewhere else after all. Just a coincidence."

He went to the door, opened it and peered into the corridor. The dim lights were still on out there. In case of fire, he assumed. He had noticed a fire escape outside at the end of the short corridor. It was reached by climbing through a window.

He closed the door again and scrambled into the top bunk.

"We'll tell her about the light bulb in the morning," he said.

They heard footsteps coming up the stairs about an hour later. At first they thought it was the warden coming to bed, but then they realised it was the sound of *two* pairs of feet. The door of the next room opened.

"Late arrivals," said Alan. "I'm surprised she let them in."

"I didn't hear their light click on, so I hope they've got a torch," said Danny. "Wonder if theirs has fused as well."

"If it has, they'll leave the door open to let in some light from the corridor, I expect."

Then the door to the room closed with a bang. They could hear two people inside moving about, as their heavy boots scraped on the wooden floor.

"Okay, so their light does work," remarked Danny. "I just didn't hear the switch."

"They're not making any effort to be quiet, are they?" said Alan.

There was no doubt about that, whoever they were. They were just stomping and banging about. From the heavy sound their boots were making, they had to be a couple of men, or youths. This was confirmed when they heard one of them talking in a low, gruff voice.

"Still safe, is it?"

"Here in my pack."

Alan whispered to Danny that the walls couldn't be very thick if they could hear every word so clearly. Danny whispered back that he expected it would be made of plaster and lath. They lay still, listening.

"Let's see it, to make sure."

There was a scuffling sound.

"Open it, then! I'll hold the candle so I can see."

"They're not supposed to have candles," said Alan as he leant out over the side of his bunk so his face was closer to Danny's.

"Nothing we can do about it," muttered Danny. "But it shows their light doesn't work either. Stop making your bed creak, or they'll hear us."

"They'll only think I'm turning over or something," replied Alan.

Then they heard:

"That's all right, then. Shut the lid. I'm going to keep the key for both of us."

"It's got to be some sort of box," decided Alan.

There was more shuffling.

"I wonder what they've got inside it," he added.

"One of them doesn't seem to trust the other very much, whatever it is," Danny whispered back.

"Wouldn't it be horrible, being with someone you didn't trust?" said Alan. "I don't see why they're together in the first place, if that's the case."

12

By now, there was silence from the next room. Alan fell asleep first, snoring gently like he always did and Danny fell asleep soon afterwards. The room was still warm from the heat left in the radiator underneath the window.

When Danny awoke, he heard the church clock from across the road striking two o'clock. At first he thought this had woken him, but then he found that it hadn't. It was the sound of voices from the next room again. There was quite a row going on in there now!

"What do you think you're doing?" someone shouted.

Then there was some sort of scuffle. It was the sound of something striking against something else, like a match against a matchbox perhaps.

"If you think you're sneaking away, you can think again. I took the liberty of locking the door while you were asleep, see?"

Alan was now awake as well. Danny heard Alan's bunk creak. Then he saw his face peering over the side at him.

"Did you hear that?" he hissed.

"Of course I did. They woke me as well."

"Where did they get a key to be able to lock the door?"

The voices from the next room were becoming even more angry.

"Thought you'd go and take the jewels for yourself, did you? I expected something like that."

Jewels? That must have been what they had been looking at earlier – in a box? But that was ridiculous! Alan crept out of his bunk and moved over to the wall, listening intently. Danny climbed out and joined him.

They both stood in their pyjamas with their ears pressed against the thin wall. In fact, with the amount of noise coming from next door, there was really no need to be standing so close.

More scuffling. Then ... "If that's how you want it! Ah, would you? Then you know what's coming to you!"

"No, Luke!" A sort of horrified gasp followed.

"That's for you!"

The two boys expected to hear the sound of a fist landing on someone's face. Instead, they heard nothing like a blow at all. That was strange. By now the moon was in a position where it had just begun to illuminate their room through the curtains, dimly but enough to make out each other and the room itself.

Then they heard another gasping sound, followed by a thud. It sounded as if one of the two in the next room had fallen to the floor.

Then more gasps.

"I'm fetching the warden," decided Alan at once, but before he could run to the door, he stepped back with a cry of sheer terror.

Danny looked to see what it was. Something was creeping across the floor towards them like an enormous slug. Except ... *it was coming out of the wall*!

Alan ran to the window and flung the curtain back. With better light in the room, they might at least be able to see what they were up against.

It wasn't a slug but a man, struggling and clawing his way across the floor. From his chest oozed a large dark stain. They could guess what that was! He gasped a final time, then lay still.

The church clock struck three into the horrified silence.

Alan and Danny pelted out of the room, shouting "Warden! Warden!" as loudly as they could. They hoped the murderer was not immediately behind them, trying to catch them too.

A few seconds later, a door opened on the floor below.

"What do you want?" they heard the warden call.

They took the stairs two at a time. The warden stood in the light of her doorway with curlers in her hair and a dark-coloured dressing-gown pulled round her.

"What's all this fuss?"

"There's a dead man – in our room!" gasped Danny.

"Then we'd better take a look, hadn't we?" said the warden, very calmly. "Come on, follow me."

She walked ahead of them, up the stairs and straight into their room. When she tried to switch on the light, of course, nothing happened.

"You should have told me the bulb's gone," she said. "Never mind, we can still see from the lights in the corridor, can't we?"

The room was empty! Alan plucked up courage and went over to his bunk to find his torch. He switched it on. There was no doubt – nothing there!

"At one time," said the warden, quite casually, "this castle became an inn. These two rooms were just one large one then. The wall was put in much later."

Then she smiled.

"So how did you like the show?" she asked.

"The show?"

"Yes. I thought, two adventurous lads would quite enjoy what goes on up here. It happens once a year, on just this one night. You're lucky, you know. Most people I book in here never see it. Just one of those things, I'm afraid."

"But ... " Alan was trying to work

something out.

"That's right. About a hundred and fifty years ago it happened. Something to do with a jewel box that a couple of men stole from the house where they were gardeners. They turned up here, pretending to be travellers. Then one of them knifed the other. Of course, the murderer got caught and hanged. And you really saw it? Did you hear it as well?"

They nodded.

"Haven't *you* seen it?" asked Danny, once he had found his voice.

"Not me. I'm not sensitive to such things." They could believe that. "But I'll show you one thing. Look here, just shine your torch."

She pulled up the edge of a mat at the side of the bunk beds, right where the man had died. There was a dark stain on the floorboards!

"That's always been there," she announced, replacing the mat over it.

"We'd rather have a different room now, if that's all right with you," murmured Alan, huskily.

The warden smiled again.

"No need for that. Once the show's over, it doesn't repeat itself – until the next year, that is. Still, I will get you another light bulb. I'll fetch the one from the room next door for you."

She came back with it, climbed onto the edge of the bunks and replaced the faulty one.

"In view of all the excitement, I think we could have breakfast a little later than usual tomorrow, eh? Give you an extra lie-in to catch up with your lost sleep."

Then she was padding off along the short corridor to the head of the stairs. Before she descended, she turned.

"Look sharp and get back into bed, then," she said. "Sleep well!"

And this time she actually laughed.

THE
GARGOYLE

T *the memory of Caleb Wilson who went no man knows where 1605.*

That was all the old stone said, propped against the wall of the church and now so weather-worn that the words could hardly be made out. It was quite small, too – more like a plaque than a proper gravestone.

"So who was Caleb Wilson?" asked Hamish, the new kid, when they pointed it out to him.

The other boys laughed.

"That's him up there," said Robert, pointing.

Hamish looked up. Just beneath the low tower of the church was a gargoyle, staring spitefully outwards. It was certainly an ugly-looking devil. What was odd, though, was that, unlike the other gargoyles, this one was not just a face, but had a complete body underneath, with a fat belly and spindly legs.

"When it rains," said Neil, "and water pours out of his mouth, it looks just as if he's being sick!"

"So who was he, then?" asked Hamish again.

"A stone mason, who disappeared in 1605. Everybody round here knows all about him."

"He can't have just disappeared."

"Well, he did. He just went and never came back and nobody heard of him again. The story is that the devil took him. Load of rubbish, of course. Most likely he just pushed off because nobody liked him."

"So why's he up there?"

"They'd been mending the roof at the time, and a gargoyle fell off. So an apprentice stone mason made that one to take its place, but he made it look just like Caleb Wilson, and that's why he's up there now."

"There's a legend about him as well," added Joe. "One of these days, he's going to come down and sort out the apprentice who made him in stone. If he can't find him, he'll make do with whoever happens to be around at the time. So the story goes, anyway."

"People have said that on dark nights, when they've been passing the church, they've actually seen old Caleb turn and look at them," commented Neil, spookily.

Hamish glanced along the road. "Would that be before or after they'd been to the pub?" he asked.

"Okay, you don't have to believe it," said Robert. He seemed pretty earnest this time. "But I'll tell you one thing, even after all these years people round here don't go near the church in the dark by themselves. There's something evil about old Caleb, so they steer clear just in case."

"Huh!" said Hamish. "That's cobblers as well."

It was stupid being scared of old churches and old churchyards. You might as well be scared of old factories and old warehouses.

Robert shrugged.

"Please yourself," he said.

"Well, hasn't anybody tried it to see what happens?"

"Tried what?"

"Going into the churchyard by themselves when it's dark, of course."

The other boys looked at each other.

"Well, there's not much point, really," said Neil. "I mean, nobody wants to hang around here when it's dark just to see what happens. It'd be ... well, boring."

"And scary," said Joe, more truthfully.

"Well, I'm not scared," retorted

Hamish. "What is there to be scared of?"

"You do it, then," said Joe. "We're not stopping you."

"I wouldn't want to stay here all night," decided Hamish. "It'd be too cold. But I'd be willing to hang about for an hour or so."

"In full view of old Caleb?" asked Neil suddenly.

"If you like."

"Half-nine to half-ten, then – tonight," decided Neil.

"You're on!" exclaimed Hamish, without hesitation.

"No matter what happens?" asked Joe slyly.

"No matter what."

"What if it's raining?" Joe looked up at the sky pointedly. The sky was already darkening with thick clouds.

"A drop of rain never hurt anybody," declared Hamish. "But what's it worth?"

The others seemed surprised.

"I mean," explained Hamish patiently, "it's a bet, isn't it? So what's the bet going to be?"

Joe, Neil and Robert consulted.

"Two quid you don't stay the full hour. That is, you're not to leave the churchyard from half-past nine to half-past ten tonight, no matter what."

"Would that be two quid each?" asked

Hamish cautiously.

They nodded.

"Okay," he agreed, satisfied.

There'd be no problem. If it did rain, he'd stay in the shelter of the church porch. They'd be up to something, of course, like rising from behind a gravestone dressed in white sheets to try to scare him off, but he'd be ready for that.

He couldn't understand the fuss. There was nothing scary about being in a churchyard at night. The bodies were underground with loads of earth on top of them. They couldn't come to the surface again, unless there was an earthquake, or a landslide or something.

A moving gargoyle just had to be nonsense. That was the trouble with these English country boys, they'd believe anything. If they had ever lived in Edinburgh, they'd be more sophisticated.

At half-past nine, he was ready. They were waiting for him at the gate of the churchyard. The rain had still not arrived, so to be on the safe side he was wearing his anorak with a hood.

"Going to stay with me, then?" he asked, jovially.

"Oh no, you're staying all by yourself. We'll be back at half-past ten," replied Neil.

"How do you know I won't nip off, then come back just before then?" Hamish wanted to know.

They were shocked.

"Of course you won't," said Joe. "That'd be cheating."

"Just testing," said Hamish, grinning.

"Right, you're to stay in the churchyard. If you go on to the road, then you've lost the bet. Agreed?" said Neil.

"Fine by me," agreed Hamish. "Be seeing you."

The other three watched him walk towards the church and stop just in front of the porch. He sat on a stone directly underneath the gargoyle of Caleb Wilson. Then the other three left him to it and wandered off down the road.

He sat there for about half an hour, feeling the whole thing was rather a waste of time. True, it was dark, but it wasn't especially cold so he loosened his anorak.

He glanced along the road towards the village pub, but could see nothing there. The village had no street lights and a high hedge obstructed any lights that might have shone from the public house.

He got up and walked up and down. Then he moved further back along the path and glanced up at the gargoyle, just visible in the gloom. If the moon should happen to appear from behind a cloud, and then more clouds moved across to obscure it again, he had no doubt it might look as if that lump of stone moved as the shadows passed over it.

So, if somebody was a bit fuddled from too much drink at the pub and happened to glance up at the church tower at a time like that, it would be easy enough to jump to the wrong conclusion. That must be the explanation, for sure.

There was a slight movement just behind him. He turned sharply to see a white shape rising from the ground near the gate and gliding towards him. What was more, there was no sound coming from it at all.

Still, there wouldn't be any sound if somebody were gliding carefully over the grass round the graves. It would have been different if whoever it was had been walking on the gravel path.

Hamish ran towards it, grabbed the white sheet and pulled.

"Just checking," said Neil, cheerfully.

"Aye, well, I'm still here," he laughed.

"Look – look there!" cried Neil, looking really frightened at something behind Hamish. He ran off.

Hamish turned to see a glowing face appear for a moment in the church porch before disappearing again.

"Come on!" Neil yelled from the gate. "Run for it Hamish!" Then, without waiting for his friend, he belted off down the road.

Oh yes, thought Hamish. Once he stepped outside the churchyard, it would cost him six pounds, and he didn't intend to be caught that way. He dropped to the ground immediately, then wriggled his way behind the gravestones until he was almost at the stone where he had first been sitting.

The lit face appeared again, just briefly, grinning wildly. Hamish pounced.

"Old trick," he grinned, "to shine a light under your chin. You won't frighten me like that."

Joe walked off rather disappointed at being caught out so easily.

"You're going to lose your bet, you know," Hamish called after him. "Better get your money ready."

"We'll see," Joe called.

There was bound to be one more trick to come, he realised. Robert was still around somewhere. So whatever was going to happen next would be down to him.

Then the storm broke, totally without warning, with lightning flashing through the pouring rain and the crash of thunder almost immediately afterwards. That meant the storm was directly overhead. Now that could be dangerous, Hamish knew. He'd better not be struck by lightning. So he dashed into the shelter of the church porch.

There was a sudden crash, very close. It sounded as if the church had been struck by lightning and something had fallen off. He peered out cautiously to see what it might be.

It was the old gargoyle, lying on its side on the ground.

He stepped out of the doorway for a moment to look up into the rain. Old Caleb had broken clean off! Good job he hadn't been directly underneath when that happened. What was more, the gargoyle hadn't even cracked. The evil-looking face was still intact on top of the protruding body and skinny legs.

He returned to the safety of the porch. There was a stone bench running down the side. Hamish sat on that and waited. At least that chunk of stone wasn't going to move and look at him. He knew exactly where it was – lying on the ground just round the corner of the church porch.

The storm passed as suddenly as it had begun. Hamish was pretty sure the other three boys would be sheltering somewhere nearby. In about half an hour, he would have won his bet. Money for old rope. Robert wasn't likely to come back to trick him now, whatever it was he'd intended to do.

Suddenly, he was aware of a movement somewhere nearby in the darkness. He was on his guard at once. Third trick coming up after all. He'd soon put a stop to that.

"Okay," he said, jumping out.

"Job Benson?" said a voice. There was a figure coming towards him. It looked like the figure of a boy.

It was a hollow-sounding voice, a curious, cavernous sound, as if it was coming out of a hollow stone. He would like to bet that somebody was speaking into a glass or a vase to make a sound like that.

"And who's Job Benson?" he asked, grabbing at the small figure in front of him.

"Job Benson the apprentice," the voice echoed. "The Job Benson I swore to be avenged upon, who placed me on the church tower."

That was strange. This kid was much too fat to be Robert!

"Take me to where he lies," intoned the voice. "Take me to him, *now!*"

Then a hand reached out and grabbed Hamish by the wrist. It was a very hard, cold hand which pulled him into the open. This trick was really being done extremely well. They must have gone to a great deal of trouble in such a short time.

Next moment, Hamish found himself face to face with the figure, and gasped. He couldn't help himself. In front of him, in the dim light, leered the unmistakable face of the gargoyle and, what was more, the lips were moving!

"Take me to Job Benson," commanded the voice.

Hamish glanced round to see where the others were. There was nobody – nobody at all. What was worse, there was no longer a stone statue on the ground where the gargoyle had fallen!

He took hold of the hand which gripped his wrist, trying to prise the fingers off. The hand was solid. When he thumped the figure in front of him, the clothes did not give way as they should have done. The entire body really seemed to be made of stone!

"I don't know Job Benson," cried Hamish, rattled now. The joke had gone far enough. "Let go of me!"

Instead, the grip tightened. It was hurting now. He was sure it was beginning to crush the bones in his wrist. This was no boy, but an evil little man. But there was no evil little man, apart from the gargoyle which had stood at the corner of the church tower only a few minutes before ...

"I will be avenged," said the hollow voice from within the stone figure. "I have waited long enough."

The accent sounded strange, too, not like the local people had now.

Hamish panicked. "I don't know any Job Benson!" he shouted. "Let go of me!"

"You still there?" he heard Neil call to him. "Time's about up."

"Come and help me!" yelled Hamish in a real panic now.

Three boys ran up. The figure of Caleb Wilson turned towards them. They hesitated, startled for a moment, then Joe grabbed the figure by the neck, Neil seized the arm which was holding Hamish, while Robert flung himself at the legs. There was a crash as the gargoyle fell forwards onto the ground.

Hamish collapsed backwards and landed heavily on the wall of the church, dazed for a few seconds. When he struggled to his feet, they could see he was still trying to free his wrist of something clinging to it.

Joe shone his torch. The hand which had been holding Hamish had broken off, but was still firmly clutched round his wrist.

What was even odder was the human bone, clearly visible, protruding from inside the shattered end of the arm which had belonged to Caleb Wilson, the gargoyle.

HOLIDAY ROMANCE

A boy who goes on holiday with his parents, especially if he is an only child, often finds there are only two possible alternatives.

The first is having to remain with his parents the whole time. If they decide to go for a boring walk, for instance, he is expected to go with them, no matter what he would much rather do instead. Or, when he wants to play on the beach, or go swimming, they always stay embarrassingly close by, in case he might come to some unlikely harm, or wander off with some undesirable new friend he's just met. Then he mustn't stay out too long or, if he gets wet, he must make sure he dries himself properly afterwards, that sort of thing.

The alternative is for the boy to let his

parents know, quite firmly, where he intends going and then go, leaving them to their own devices while he does something more interesting.

This is only possible, however, if his parents are rather more sensible than the first example. Fortunately, Andy's parents were.

On holiday, they let him do whatever he liked.

What they didn't know, because Andy hadn't told them and because he'd only just found out himself, was that quite unexpectedly, girls had started to find him remarkably attractive. Almost like flies round a jam pot, he decided.

Whenever he turned out with the school football team, for instance, girls of all shapes, sizes and ages would be on the touch-line, cheering for him and nobody else. In class, some girl or other could always be relied on to pass him sweets, or a note asking if he would go out with her.

He wasn't bad looking, he decided, as he inspected himself in the full-length mirror in his hotel room. It was soon after breakfast on the first morning of the holiday. He was just wearing his swimming trunks at the time, trying to see exactly what it was that girls saw in him.

His hair was dark and slightly curly, his eyes were brown with long lashes, and he was neither too fat nor too skinny. Perhaps, it was these attributes that the girls found attractive, but, he couldn't be sure.

Because the girls seemed to be so interested in him, he had discovered that he had become just as fascinated by them. It wasn't that they were more fun than boys, they were just – different.

Now he had finished examining himself, he decided he'd go out. So, just as he was, he went down to the entrance hall, where he knew his parents would be.

"Going to the beach," he said to his parents, who were in conversation with another couple at the time.

"Need a towel?" asked his father, noticing his swimming trunks.

"No, shan't bother. I'll soon get dry," Andy replied. "See you later."

"About one o'clock, then," called his mother. "If you want anything to eat."

"Okay."

"What a nice boy," he heard the other woman remark as he was leaving. "I suppose he's your son?"

He wasn't surprised at her reaction. It was always the same nowadays. Even very old ladies he met in the street invariably smiled at him. A while ago he wouldn't have approved of all this female attention, but now he was a little older, he was finding it quite acceptable.

After leaving the hotel, Andy strode

confidently down the path to the big beach in front of it and across the soft sand. He sat by himself for a moment at the water's edge, hands clasped round his knees, while he slowly looked round to size up the prospects. He didn't need to.

"Hello," said a girl almost immediately, coming up behind him.

He turned his head. She was one of a group of three.

"Hello," he said, not impressed by any of them.

"Do you mind if we sit here?" she persisted.

"Can if you like," he replied.

They didn't look the type who actually wanted to go into the water, so the best way to get rid of them was obvious. As they sat down, he got up, walked into the water and struck out. He swam back again much farther along the beach. He was relieved they hadn't decided to follow him along the sands.

This was more hopeful because there were more people on this stretch of beach. A group of boys were kicking a ball about. In the shallows, a young boy and girl had stopped paddling and were kicking water at each other. Some small children were building sand castles with their buckets and spades. Various adults were either in the sea, sunning themselves, or keeping a watchful eye on their children. One fat woman had even gone topless. Urgh!

Then, as he was pushing his hair back from his face, he saw her.

Everyone else, like himself, was dressed for the beach. But this girl was different, absolutely amazing.

She was fully and expensively dressed and, she was gorgeous, with long blond hair sweeping down to her shoulders. She was also about his own age.

He watched her stroll along the beach and disappear behind a sand dune. What was especially intriguing about her, apart from the way she was dressed, was that as she passed by she had looked at him, briefly, and that was all, just a passing glance. Andy, however, had taken a much longer look at her.

Never one to resist a challenge, he started to stroll in the same direction, climbed the slight rise of the sand dune and came down on the other side. Since she wasn't there, he carried on over the next one. That's where he found her laying with her back against the dune just below him. He descended slowly.

"Hello," he said. "I didn't expect to find anyone else here."

He flopped down at the side of her.

"Why are you dressed like that?" he asked.

The direct approach, he had learned from experience, was often best. It showed interest.

"This is what I always wear," she assured him. "Well, as it's hot, I'd have thought you'd want to be in bathers, or something. Like me," he added.

"I never do," she said.

Andy was pleased to notice that she seemed to be looking him over with a great deal of interest. He wondered for a moment if she had some strange skin complaint which she had to keep covered up, but since he couldn't see any sign of one, he decided that couldn't be the explanation.

"Why not?" he asked.

"Because these are the only clothes I have."

Well, that didn't make much sense, unless she had her bathers on underneath and had come here to change, expecting no one to be around while she did. Either that, or for once, a girl just wanted to get rid of him. He decided to put it to the test.

"I'll go if you like," he said.

"I don't mind if you stay, really," she replied.

That was better.

"All right, then. So why are you really dressed like that?"

"I fell off our yacht, just out there." She nodded her head towards the sea.

That didn't make sense either, nor did what she said next.

"And drowned," she added, casually. "These were the clothes I was wearing at the time. Two summers ago."

Andy stared at her.

"You look perfectly all right to me," he said.

"Well, so do you. And I expect that you feel all right as well," she added, laying a hand on his chest and keeping it there. Andy found he didn't mind in the slightest. "But of course, you're bound to feel all right, aren't you? You're alive."

"And how do I know that you aren't?" he asked. "Go on, tell me!"

"All that anyone can ever see of me, apart from my clothes, are my face and hands," she said. "And even they don't really exist. There is nothing else."

"I can feel your hand all right," he said, looking pointedly at where it still lay on his chest. "And I bet I can feel your face as well," he said for good measure, and put out his own hand to feel. He could.

"Well, of course you can. I just said."

"I think you're talking rubbish," Andy declared.

Frankly, he was getting just a bit fed up with this conversation. If it didn't get any better soon, he'd go and chat up some other girl, or find one who might chat him up. A pity such a beautiful girl had to be so weird.

"It's not rubbish at all. And I can prove it if you like."

"Oh yes," he said. "How?"

"By taking all my clothes off, of course."

Andy, naturally, was absolutely astonished, but he soon recovered his composure.

"Go on, then. I dare you," he said, grinning.

"All right, I will." She took her hand off his chest and started to unbutton her dress. That really took him by surprise.

"Wait a minute," he said, and climbed to the top of the sand dune. Then he came back down again. "It's okay, there's nobody about, but I don't believe you're really going to do it."

"I am," she replied, calmly. "But you'll have to look the other way first, and not turn round until I tell you," she instructed.

"Oh yes. And by then you'll have cleared off, won't you?" he said.

"No. I promise I'll still be here, and then you'll see exactly what I mean."

Wow! he thought in excitement. She really did mean it! He turned obediently to face the dune until she said she was ready.

"You can look now," he heard her say a few moments later, and turned round expectantly.

All her clothes lay in a heap in front of him, all right. She really had done what she said! The only thing was, she wasn't there herself!

"Now do you believe me?" he heard her say from somewhere ahead of him.

He hurried to the top of the next dune and peered over, knowing she had to be hiding on the other side. But she wasn't there either. Nobody was.

Then he knew exactly what to do to draw her into the open. He slithered back down the dune, scooped her clothes up and held them over his head.

"If you want your clothes back, you'll have to come and get them," he called. If she really hadn't got her bathers on underneath, he didn't want anyone else to hear and come to investigate.

Then, to his astonishment and horror, the clothes began to fade and disappear in his hands!

"See? What I told you really was the truth," he heard the girl saying almost right in his ear, but there was still nobody visible, apart from himself.

He managed to cling on to what looked like an underskirt as everything else vanished completely.

Then, what felt like a quick, cold wind blew past, and suddenly the underskirt was snatched out of his hands and disappeared into thin air like the rest of her clothes.

For the remainder of the holiday, to his parents' surprise and occasional annoyance, Andy decided to opt for the first alternative mentioned.

He wasn't so keen on girls afterwards, either, no matter how they tried. He decided he'd rather stick to football. It was safer!

OUT OF HER BODY

Jessica was almost asleep when she turned over to find a light shining into her eyes.

She opened them reluctantly. The street lamp across the road was shining through a gap between the curtains. She couldn't have closed them properly, so she got out of bed again to pull them closer together.

But now, somehow, the curtains didn't seem to be there any more! She could see them all right, but her hands seemed to be passing through them instead of pulling them together.

At first she thought she was dreaming. She glanced round the bedroom anxiously, to see if anything else was different or strange.

Something else certainly was!

She didn't believe it at first, until she crept cautiously towards her bed to take a closer look. There was no doubt. She could see herself fast asleep in it. She was lying on her back, breathing deeply and regularly with her mouth slightly open.

Suddenly, she felt extremely tired, but when she tried to get back into bed again, she found she couldn't feel her duvet either, and couldn't lift it up to get underneath.

So she just lay on top of it, closed her eyes again and seemed to sink back into her body. Then she really was fast asleep again.

That was a most peculiar dream, she decided when she woke the following morning. She still remembered every detail of it. She must have been dreaming because the gap in the curtains was still there, and now sunlight was shining through.

But it wasn't the sunlight which had woken her. It was her brother, Alexander, shaking her.

"Get up, Scabby," he was shouting. "I expect you forgot to set your alarm again."

He shook her again as hard as he could, even though he could see she was now awake.

Alexander was the sort of boy old women cooed over, other children invariably wanted on their side for games, and even the teachers smiled at encouragingly. Everyone's favourite. It had been like that ever since he was born. It just wasn't fair. Other people just didn't know what he was *really* like.

It had been little more than a week since he had deliberately tripped her over in the street. She had fallen full-length and grazed her chin on the pavement. The scab was still there. He knew that reminding her of it upset her, which was why he kept on doing it. He was like that.

Now he grabbed hold of her duvet in both hands and dragged it halfway to the door before running off downstairs.

"Is Jessica up yet?" asked his mother.

"Suppose so," he grunted, starting on his breakfast.

"Then go and call her, or she'll be late for school," she told him.

"Breakfast's ready, Scabby, so hurry up!" he yelled, without bothering to leave the table.

"Tell him to stop calling me that," said Jessica angrily, as she came down a few minutes later.

"He doesn't mean anything by it," said their mother, indulgently.

"Oh, yes he does!" snorted Jessica.

She could tell that he was being spiteful from the way he was smiliing at her. Not the friendly smile he always put on for everyone else, but the mocking grin he reserved especially for her. She wished she could have marked *his* face as well, just to see how he would feel about being teased all the time.

The next night, as she was dropping off to sleep, she thought she had better be certain she had set her alarm this time.

She sat up in bed and peered at the illuminated clock on the table beside her. The little green dot was glowing at the side of the time display, so she had obviously done it.

Then she realised she was having the same dream as before! Beneath her, her body hadn't moved. It was almost as if she was really sitting up out of it.

She got out of bed at once. At least, she thought she did, until she realised she was watching herself breathing quietly in bed, exactly the same as the previous night.

She stood absolutely still in shock for a moment. She decided not to panic. Whatever this was, it was hardly a nightmare. It would only become one if she found she couldn't get back into her body again at the end of it.

She lay back on top of her bed, exactly as she had done the last time, and waited for whatever was going to happen next.

What she did notice was how little she seemed to weigh. The body underneath her didn't even stir, even though she was lying directly on top of it.

The next thing she knew, it was

morning again and music was coming from her radio alarm.

"Sleep well, Scabby?" asked Alexander, poking his nose round the door.

"Perfectly," she said, coldly. Without giving him chance to say anything else, she dashed into the bathroom.

As she dried herself, she decided not to mention this to anybody else. If Alexander got to hear of her strange experience, as he was bound to if she told her parents, she'd never hear the last of it. Pretty soon it would be all over the school. Alexander would make sure of that.

At least her chin was almost back to normal. She looked at her face in the mirror and carefully eased the last scab from it. Alexander wouldn't be able to call her that name for very much longer. She put a little cream on to help hide the red mark which still remained.

The next night was even more interesting. She was just beginning to doze off when she realised that this might be the clue. On both previous occasions, the strange dream had started at the very moment she thought she was about to drop off to sleep.

So, simply as an experiment, she got out of bed immediately, walked slowly to the door, then just as slowly back towards her bed.

Just as she expected! She hadn't taken

her body with her. It was still lying there, fast asleep.

How far, she wondered, would it be safe to go? To the door, perhaps? She had just done that. So what if she went further, say right outside the room – would she still be able to get back again? And what would happen if she couldn't?

Jessica decided to risk it, just this once. Everyone left their bedroom doors partly open when they went to bed. It was a habit, from the time she and Alexander had both been little so their parents could hear them if they woke unexpectedly.

She walked over to the door and tried to open it wider, but she encountered the same problem as she had when she tried to close her curtains and lift up her duvet – she simply couldn't move it. With some difficulty, she squeezed her way through the narrow gap instead. Then she stood outside the door for a moment.

All right so far, she thought, as she eased her way back into her room again. That had been safe enough. Her body still seemed to be asleep. She went over to her bed to make quite sure.

Now she slipped out for a second time. She padded along the passage to the next bedroom – Alexander's. She eased her way past his partially-open door and crept towards his bed.

When she peered down at him, he was obviously fast asleep.

She wondered ... if he did happen to wake just at that moment, would he be able to see her? Probably not, she decided.

After all, it could only be her own "ghost" standing in his room. She wasn't really there, so she would almost certainly be completely invisible to him.

This was an absolutely amazing discovery. She wondered how many other people had found what could happen in that brief moment each night before falling asleep. Very few, she suspected.

While she was standing next to him, she did try giving Alexander's hateful face a hard slap to see if it would wake him up. She had wanted to slap it for a very long time. To her regret, her hand simply slid through him, like the hand of a real ghost.

Next she tried punching him really hard in the stomach. That had no effect either. She tried again, very much harder, several times.

Rather to her surprise, on her fourth attempt, she felt just a slight resistance. On the next blow, she was sure a little indentation actually appeared in the bedclothes. Now that, she decided, was really exciting!

The familiar feeling of tiredness suddenly came over her. She hurried back to her own room, slipped through the gap in the door and lay down at once. After all, she didn't want to risk not being able to get back to her body.

"Sleep well?" she asked the next morning, bursting into Alexander's room like he always did when she was still asleep.

But, she found that this morning, Alexander was already sitting up in bed. He was looking at her rather oddly.

"Of course," he said, and got out of bed. "Why shouldn't I?"

"No reason," she said.

But there was a reason. She had managed to make his duvet move, even if only slightly. And next time ... !

The next time, after emerging from her room, she went into the bathroom first. The door of that was always left wide open. She tried to turn on one of the taps. There was no way she could make it move.

"Too difficult yet," she said aloud to herself. Then she realised what she had done and wondered whether anyone else could have heard her.

She thought she had better find out. She slipped across to Alexander's room, bent over and shouted his name right in his ear. He didn't even stir. Good! Another useful thing she had discovered.

Trying to turn a bathroom tap on had been a mistake, though. She should have tried something easier first. She went back to her own room.

She was delighted to find that she could make her curtains sway a little, as if in a gentle breeze, even if she still couldn't pull them open yet.

As that tired feeling came over her again, there was a faint smile on her face as she lay down on the bed and finally fell asleep.

"What are you doing?" asked Alexander.

It was the following evening, just before he went to bed. He had barged into her room without even knocking first, as usual.

"Mind your own business," said Jessica.

"Why have you got all those pens and pencils out on your dressing-table?" he persisted.

"Counting them," she lied.

She had been carefully weighing them in her hand before Alexander had come in. Now they were lined up in order with the lightest at one end and the heaviest at the other.

"Well, that's not your pen, it's mine!" declared Alexander, snatching one up. At the same time, he deliberately knocked the rest of them to the floor.

She didn't bother chasing after him. She could afford to be patient now. She picked them all up from the carpet and started again.

Later that night, when she rose from her bed, she concentrated on picking up the first in the line, a slim little pencil she had taken from the back of an old diary.

At first nothing happened. She couldn't even feel it was there. She concentrated harder and tried again. And again. Then, with sudden excitement, she realised she was putting her fingers round it. Next, she was picking it up! It rose into the air as easily as if she had been holding it in her real hand.

After that, the rest seemed easy. Even the heavy old fountain pen, which had once been her grandfather's, floated upwards effortlessly.

She got up and went to her bedroom curtains. They were no problem now, either. She managed to open and close them several times before that tired feeling took over and she had to sink back into her bed again.

She discovered Alexander was up early when she went into his room, hoping to give him a good shaking to wake him up. For some reason, there was a little pile of books on the carpet at the side of his bed.

"Just been sorting out a few things," he said, suddenly appearing in the doorway behind her.

"That dictionary's mine, you little

wretch! she exclaimed, noticing it about halfway down the pile and plucking it out. She had wondered where it had gone.

"You leave my things alone!"

"You'd got my pen," he called after her.

"That was quite different, and you know it," she shouted back, angrily.

"Scabby!" she heard him jeer, just before she got back to her room.

That settled it, she thought, as she slammed the dictionary back on the shelf next to her bed. She knew exactly what she intended to do now!

That night, she no longer had to squeeze her way out past her bedroom door. She simply pulled it open. Just as she had expected. A little more practice and, before long, she would be ready for what she now had in mind.

She went downstairs to the kitchen. It would be a much better idea to try to turn on one of the taps down there than in the bathroom. From downstairs, the sound of running water was less likely to be heard than upstairs; if she really did manage to turn it on, that was.

She did manage it, easily, and turned it off again. No trouble at all. She turned it on and off a few more times. Then she paused because she was sure she could hear someone talking.

She listened carefully for a moment, before realising it was only the television in the living room. Her parents must have forgotten to switch it off before they had gone to bed. It must have been on all the time. With her mind on other things, she simply hadn't noticed it before.

Suddenly, the sound stopped. When she went to investigate, she found the television wasn't switched on at all. She must have been hearing the one from next door instead. They always went to bed late.

However, since she was in the living room, she thought she might as well see if she was now capable of picking up one of the dining chairs. She went over to one and was just reaching out to it – when it suddenly rose into the air all by itself!

When she stepped back in surprise, it immediately lowered itself to the carpet again.

This was totally unexpected, and dangerous. To be able to make things move was one thing, but for them to move just because she happened to be near them was quite another.

She regarded the chair cautiously, in case it was going to do it again. It didn't – not even when she moved her hands towards it. The next time it rose into the air, it really was because she was picking it up.

She went quickly back to her room.

Once inside, she closed the door behind her. Then she picked up the teddy bear she had had since she was a little girl and squeezed it fiercely in both hands, scrunching its body until it was a shapeless mess.

She barely had time to push it under her bed before she felt so tired she simply had to lie down. However, that feeling was much longer in coming this time. She felt pleased about this before she finally drifted into sleep.

In the morning, her bedroom door was still firmly shut.

When she dragged her teddy out from under the bed, it was still thoroughly mangled. Good! Absolute proof that she hadn't been dreaming. She really *was* able to leave her body! So now she was ready.

She hid the teddy right at the back of the cupboard, where no one was likely to find it. She was in a very happy frame of mind. She didn't even make a fuss when Alexander deliberately spilled hot coffee over her hand at breakfast. She was looking forward to the expected moment all day.

When she knew it had arrived, she rose from her bed at once. At the door, she paused and looked back to make quite sure she hadn't got out too soon. No, her timing was perfect. Her body was still lying there. She walked slowly along the passage to Alexander's room.

As she had expected, he was fast asleep. She bent over him, eased her fingers gently round the back of his neck, placed both thumbs against his throat, and squeezed.

She was really going to enjoy this, feeling him squirm beneath her hands as he woke up. Then he would struggle hopelessly as he gasped for air and, after a few more minutes, finally lie completely still.

He had it coming to him. Besides, no one would ever suspect her. After all, she wasn't really there. She was asleep in her own bed the whole time.

But, something was going terribly wrong! Somehow, her hands seemed to be round her own throat, not Alexander's. *She* was the one who was really suffocating and gasping for air.

Even when she let go of him and backed right away from the bed, those hands were still clamped round her throat, pressing and squeezing.

She was barely able to breathe. That was when she realised – *they weren't her hands*.

It suddenly came to her. The way Alexander had piled those books at the side of his bed, with a slim paperback on top then increasingly thicker books all the way down to a heavy encyclopaedia at the bottom ... the television ... the chair that had moved by itself.

With growing terror, she recognised a familiar pattern. Choking for breath, she staggered the short distance to her own room – desperate to get back in time.

She almost fell through the wide open door to see herself writhing on the bed, silently fighting off the invisible hands as she struggled for air.

Just before the figure on the bed lay quite still and she finally faded away, she thought she saw something that wasn't really Alexander slip past her towards his own room.

But it was now, of course, too late.

SARDINES

"Come along, children," called Mrs Merton, brightly. "We're going to play sardines."

It was nice of Mrs Merton to have invited them all to the party. She had certainly taken a great deal of trouble over everything.

The problem was she had little idea of what children of their age wanted. Most of the games would have gone down very well with six-years-olds!

Nevertheless, each of them had dutifully been blindfolded and had tried to pin a tail to a cardboard donkey with hilarious results. Well, it was hilarious to Mrs Merton at any rate, who laughed uproariously each time the tail finished up on the donkey's nose, or one of its legs, or wherever.

Then, playing Hunt the Treasure, they had each been give a much too easy clue written on a piece of paper. This led them to more easy clues in other parts of the house, or its enormous garden, and finally to the prize, which had been hidden in the low branches of a tree.

Tony had won that, mainly because he had run the fastest. He scowled when he found it was a little chocolate rabbit tied up in a pink ribbon.

They had drunk lots of pop and had helped themselves to the lavish buffet. Now they were going to play sardines.

It wasn't really the sort of party any of them would have chosen to go to. It was too organised, with too much activity, too much of being told what they were going to enjoy and then having to enjoy it just to please Mrs Merton. Mrs Merton was quite clearly out of touch with their age-group.

"What's sardines?" asked Robert, stuffing the last cream cake into his mouth.

"Little fishes you buy in a tin," said George.

"It's rather like hide-and-seek," replied Mrs Merton. "Only when you find the one who's hiding, you stay there until you're all packed into the same place – like sardines you know."

"We shan't really be like sardines," said George, thoughtfully. "Sardines are packed head to tail, not head to head."

Mrs Merton ignored him.

"Now, who shall we have to start us off?" she asked. "Would you like to, Alice?"

"All right," said Alice, not over-enthusiastically.

"There is one thing," announced Mrs Merton. "As most of you probably know, the house has a cellar. The steps are very steep and can be dangerous. So I've put a big notice on the door warning you not to go in. There was once a nasty accident."

"What happened?" asked Robert, suddenly interested.

"It was many years ago now, when I held my very first children's party," said Mrs Merton, hesitantly. "One of the girls ... um ... opened the cellar door by mistake and fell down the steps."

"Did she die?"

"Yes. But I don't think we should dwell on that, do you, Robert?" said Mrs Merton, quickly. "It was very nasty at the time and almost put me off holding any more parties, but then I thought, if everyone was really sensible ... Anyway, enough of that. Let's play sardines, shall we?"

Mrs Merton wasn't a bad sort at all, everyone knew that. She always took the leading role whenever they needed to raise funds for local events. She contributed to a great many charities and had even paid for a new village hall when the old one began to fall down.

Each year, on her birthday, she invited the children of the village to a party.

She was lonely, George decided, that was why. It was all very well living in a large house with lots of servants, but she didn't really mix very much with other people.

Still, it was a pity she didn't find out more about what sort of party they'd really like to have. The local children came more out of a sense of duty than anything else when they got the letters on headed notepaper, inviting them.

"So are you ready?" asked Mrs Merton.

Alice nodded.

"Then off you go! We'll close our eyes and count to five hundred, slowly. You can hide anywhere in the house or grounds – except the cellar, of course. We don't want a repeat of the unfortunate accident, do we?"

Alice ran off.

There were nine of them in all. It was only a small village, and once anyone reached the age of fourteen Mrs Merton, who always seemed to know when their birthdays were, sent a little present but never invited them again.

She never invited children who were too young, either. She didn't want little ones spoiling the fun for the rest, as she had once explained to a mother who was rather put out that little Tommy hadn't been invited. He wouldn't be invited, Mrs Merton had said, until he was old enough.

Tommy, who was George's young brother, *was* old enough now. He was at the party this year with the rest of them. He peeked through his fingers to see which way Alice went.

"Four hundred and ninety-nine, five hundred!" declared Mrs Merton finally. "Off you go!"

Most of the others ran towards the trees and shrubs at the far end of the big garden. It was the obvious place to search first since there were plenty of good hiding places amongst the undergrowth, but Tommy ran towards the house and in through the open kitchen door instead.

"You're getting warm," smiled Mrs Merton's cook encouragingly as she stacked empty dishes into the dishwasher.

Alice had passed her only a minute or two before, she told him.

Tommy smiled happily back at her as he ran through the kitchen and into the house.

In the hallway, he paused. He had just passed the door into the cellar. He knew it was the cellar because of the big notice on white paper which Mrs Merton had pinned to it. A wide staircase swept upwards in front of him.

Now would he hide somewhere downstairs if he was the one doing the hiding? That would make it too easy, he decided, especially when he didn't know his way around the house.

Alice did know her way around because she'd been to Mrs Merton's parties before. He bet that last year, whoever had been the one to hide, had gone straight up the stairs.

So, if Alice had any sense, she wouldn't do the same this year. Therefore, she would have found somewhere to hide downstairs instead, he reasoned.

He opened the first door he came to on the left. Obviously it was the dining room because of the big wooden table in the middle with lots of chairs round it. Nowhere for a good hiding place in there. He shut that door and went on to the next.

A drawing room or sitting room or something, a bit like their own front room but much bigger, of course. He looked around quickly. Not enough space behind any of the chairs in there for anyone to hide, either.

He closed that door behind him, walked across the hall and opened the door directly opposite.

A study, he supposed, with a big desk and a thick leather chair, and big bookcases full of books lining the walls. There was one bookcase right behind the desk, though, that looked a bit different from all the others.

Tommy tiptoed towards it. Now he could see why it was different. It didn't quite fit. And there was a little catch at the side of one of the books. When he moved it, just to see what happened, he found the bookcase was really a door to a little dark room with no windows in it.

He looked in, saw her hiding there, and ran back to the door to the hallway. He closed it quietly, then shot back into the little secret room and pulled the door shut behind them.

"Alice?"

"Yes?"

"I've shut the door into the hall so the others won't guess where we are," he whispered.

There was a prize for the first person to find Alice, he knew that. Well, he'd won it already, he thought with satisfaction.

"Keep very quiet, then," said Alice, "or they might hear us."

So Tommy kept very quiet. It was dark in there. He was glad he wasn't alone.

Then there was silence, but not for long.

"I can't hear them coming," said Tommy. "I expect they're still searching."

He opened the concealed door a crack, which let a little light into the room. He could see Alice standing in the corner. He listened carefully for a moment before pulling the door towards him again.

"I think they've realised you're not outside," he whispered. "I think I can hear them going up the stairs."

"That's what I thought they'd do," said Alice, "which is why I didn't hide up there."

"That's what I thought, too," said Tommy happily. He was glad he'd been right about where not to hide.

The trouble was, they didn't come down again. Tommy began to grow impatient. What on earth could they be doing up there?

"How long are we supposed to wait?" he asked.

"Until they find where we are and join us, of course," said Alice.

So Tommy carried on waiting. After quite some time, he was surprised to hear them calling his name.

"Tommy! Where are you? Come on out, it's all over now," That was Tony. It sounded as if he was in the study, just on the other side of the concealed door.

"I bet he's gone in there," he heard his brother George say.

Then the concealed door was flung open.

"Why have you been hiding in there

all this time?" George demanded.

"You were supposed to join me," retorted Tommy. "And why is the game over?"

"Because we've all found Alice, of course. She was hiding under the big bed in Mrs Merton's bedroom."

"But she's been in here with me all the ... "

Then Tommy saw Alice standing just behind the rest of them, smirking, with a worried-looking Mrs Merton next to her. He counted. Including himself, that would make ten children, not nine.

He turned round. The secret room was completely empty.

"Well, she said here name was Alice," he said, crossly.

"That was also the name of the girl who fell down the cellar steps all those years ago," muttered Mrs Merton, just before she fainted.

Needless to say, Sardines was not one of the games played at Mrs Merton's birthday party the following year.

INVISIBLE!

The house had been derelict for years. It was going to be demolished, everyone said. It stood by itself in a large overgrown garden behind a crumbling old brick wall. The windows were boarded up and part of the roof had started to sag – there seemed to be nothing right with it any more. It deserved to be demolished.

Then one day, as James was on his paper round, he noticed workmen on the roof putting in new joists and tiles. Then the boards came down and new window frames were put in. Before long there was a fresh coat of paint and bright, new curtains hanging at the windows.

The whole thing only seemed to have taken about a day from start to finish, which was very fast going, thought James.

The house stood at the very end of his paper round. So every afternoon he walked along to the gate, just on the off-chance of seeing whoever it was who now lived there.

There was always a chance that they might want newspapers delivered. Mr Grimes, the newsagent, gave extra cash at the end of a week if any of his newspaper delivery boys or girls found a new customer for him.

James never saw anybody, though, so after a few days of walking up to the gate before going home with his empty bag, he decided he ought to make a move. This time, James opened the gate, walked right up to the front door, and knocked.

"Do come round to the back," he heard a voice call. It was a woman's voice.

When he reached the back door, she was standing there smiling, obviously waiting for him to explain himself. She seemed a nice young woman.

"I wondered," said James hesitantly, "if you'd like me to deliver your newspapers." He'd never actually plucked up courage to ask anyone before.

"Now that is a good idea," she said. "Just the local evening paper, though. Will that be all right?"

"Of course." James had not expected it to be so easy. He thought that she would have already ordered her papers from Saint's, the other newsagents.

"There's just one thing," she added as he turned to go. "I don't want it pushed through the letterbox. I want you to bring it right in here, into the kitchen, and put it on the table."

James was agreeable. It sounded a little unusual, but if that was what she wanted ...

"What if you're not in?" he asked.

"I shall be," the young woman assured him. "I shall always be in when you call."

It was almost as if she had emphasised the word *you*. In fact, he was sure of it. He felt rather flattered.

"Start tomorrow, then," the young woman said. "And don't knock, just walk straight in."

The following evening, leaving her house until last, because after all it was the furthest from the shop, he dutifully opened the gate at the end of the garden and walked round to the kitchen door. Then he hesitated. Perhaps he really should knock first. But then, she had told him quite clearly not to.

So he tried the door, and as it opened to his touch, walked inside boldly and laid a copy of the *Evening Mail* on the kitchen table, folding it neatly first.

It was a strange sort of kitchen. Round the walls were open shelves almost as high as the ceiling. Most of them held bottles and jars filled with all kinds of herbs. There were rows of them.

A plain wooden table stood in the centre of the room, with two chairs next to it. In a corner by the window was a sink and draining board, a cooker next to that and, most unusual of all, an open fireplace on the other side of the kitchen with something bubbling away in a large saucepan.

Then the door to the rest of the house opened and the same young woman was standing there smiling at him.

"Ah, the newspaper," she said. "Now don't forget, every evening just place it on the table. If the door's closed, as it usually will be, don't bother to knock, walk straight in. It'll be quite all right."

This continued for several evenings. James had no idea why she wanted her newspaper brought inside, instead of being pushed through the letterbox. He thought that perhaps there was a dog in the house, which might chew it up before she had read it, but he'd never heard one barking, and she seemed to live by herself anyway.

As James continued to leave the newspaper on the kitchen table each day, the young woman would come in smiling, as if she had been waiting for him.

Now it was Friday evening.

"Since I feel I know you so well now, would you like a cup of tea?" she asked brightly.

"Yes, please," he said. After all, he was in no hurry, since she was the last customer on his round. "I ought to have your name on my card," he added, fumbling for it in his pocket and taking out a pencil at the same time. After all, Mr Grimes would need to know that.

"It's Miss Warner," she replied. "Brenda Warner. And what's your name?" she asked, as he wrote it down.

"James," he said.

"A very nice name, James," she commented thoughtfully. "It seems to suit you, somehow. Now sit down while I get you that cup of tea."

He sat on one of the chairs, dropping his empty delivery bag on the floor. She sat opposite him as soon as she had produced two cups and poured the tea. Then she added a little sugar to his.

"You won't need milk," she continued, "and you'll find it a very pleasant taste indeed, but perhaps not quite one which you'd expect."

He sipped it. It did taste different ... definitely tea, but with a most unusual flavour.

"I see you're looking at my jars and things," noticed Miss Warner. "Well, I might

as well tell you, I'm something of a herbalist.
You're drinking herbal tea, in fact."

"Is that what you do for a living, Miss
Warner?" asked James. "Being a herbalist?"

"Since I'm calling you James, you can
call me Brenda," said Miss Warner. "There's
no need for either of us to stand on ceremony,
is there?" She crossed her slender legs, very
languidly.

"No, I wouldn't really say I'm a
herbalist, but herbs and potions are my
hobby. I can do wonders with them. I grow
many of them in the garden, you know."

So that explained why the garden of
this smart house looked as if it was still
growing nothing but weeds. They were really
Brenda's herbs. That was obvious now.

"In fact," she continued thoughtfully,
"I can do unbelievable things with herbs."

"Like what?" asked James.

"Let's just say that in the old days I'd
probably have been labelled as a witch," she
said, and laughed. It was a really tinkling
laugh, a very cheery sound.

James laughed as well, more out of
politeness than anything.

"For instance, what would you do if
you were invisible?" she asked him.

"You what?" said James, wondering if
he had heard her properly.

"What would you do if you were
invisible?" she asked again.

72

James thought. It would be fun, he was sure of that. If nobody could see him, he could take things from shops without paying for them. He could have free seats at the cinema – though it might be a bit awkward if somebody came and sat on him, not knowing he was there. He could wander about and see what other people were doing when they didn't think anyone could see them. It might be fun at school as well!

"Stealing from shops would not be a good idea," she remarked. "People would see the objects moving, even if they couldn't see you. And sneaking into a cinema would be all very well, but you have to realise that while people couldn't see you, they would still feel you if you touched them, and you'd have to touch somebody to get to a seat, wouldn't you? No, I think you'd have to treat it as a bit of fun – wandering about and watching, that sort of thing."

Then she said something very surprising.

"I can make you invisible, if you like. The effect will only last for an hour or so, but I really can do it."

"Go on, then," said James, humouring her. Did she think he was a little kid, trying to make him believe that sort of nonsense? Or was she ... not quite all there? "Do it now. I bet you can't."

"No ... not now. Come back later. Shall

we say, seven o'clock? Then I'll prove it to you."

"All right," he said. Whatever she was going to prove, it would be interesting to see her try.

He did have second thoughts, though. You shouldn't go to places with people you don't know. It might be very dangerous. But then, she was only a young woman, quite obviously living by herself, so he couldn't see himself coming to much harm. It should be all right.

So, at seven o'clock he was back, out of his school clothes and dressed in his casuals. He wondered on his way there whether this was going to be something he could boast about at school afterwards. Normally he never had anything to boast about.

He walked into the kitchen without bothering to knock, because after all she had told him to do that when he delivered the paper. He would like to bet, though, that the whole thing was going to be a big disappointment and a waste of time. Things usually turned out that way for James.

She was already there waiting for him.

"Okay," he said, trying not to sound too eager, "what am I supposed to do?"

"Just sit in that chair," she said.

Then she went to the bubbling liquid in the saucepan over the open fire and dipped a mug into it, and placed it half-full on the table in front of him. James looked inside. It was a brown-looking liquid, with some green bits floating on top.

"When that's cool enough," she said, "drink it."

"What's in it?" He was just a little suspicious now.

"I'm not going to tell you, James, but I can assure you that it won't do you any harm at all."

He took a tiny sip, and found that whatever it was, tasted sweet, rather like a sweet sherry which had been heated up. He'd once tasted sherry, but hadn't liked it much.

"All of it, once it's cooled," she instructed, watching him.

He drank the rest in one gulp soon afterwards. Then he waited for a moment to see if he felt any different, but he didn't. He remained still, with Brenda standing in front of him. She was watching his face intently.

"Now you're completely invisible," she announced.

"Yes. Well. I think I'd better be going now," he said. She was obviously a loony after all!

Without a word Brenda left the kitchen and returned with a small hand mirror.

"All right," she said. "Look into that

and tell me what you see."

When James glanced in the mirror, he had a fright. He could see the wall behind him and the reflection of the shelves and bottles and jars, and the outside door – but he had no head! He grabbed the mirror and twisted it in all directions. He discovered that he could not see his hand where it should have been holding the handle of the mirror, either! He simply wasn't there!

"And what conclusion do you come to?" Brenda asked him, casually.

"I'm completely invisible!" This was exciting, no doubt about it. He was glad he'd come now.

"Yes," she said calmly, "but I think you might have noticed just one tiny problem."

He tilted the mirror again, and instantly saw what it was. He could see his empty clothes moving about with nobody inside them!

"To be completely invisible," Brenda was saying, "you must take all your clothes off."

"I don't think so," he said, embarrassed.

"Why not? No one can possibly see you. Even I can't. All anyone can see at the moment are your clothes."

James put the mirror down on the table, and looked down at himself. It made sense. He just couldn't be seen, not even by himself, so it had to be all right.

It seemed strange to be removing his clothes while somebody was watching him, but of course Brenda was unable to see him anyway. So he took them off one by one and folding them neatly, laid them in a pile on the table, with his trainers on top.

"I like the way you're so neat," Brenda complimented him. "I noticed how neat you were the first time you laid a nice-folded newspaper on my table. Now where are you?"

She found his shoulders and held him still, at arm's length.

"Right," she said, "let me give you some necessary advice. If it rains, the water will make your outline show, so you mustn't go outside and expect to remain unseen when it's raining. Also, if you tread in mud, your footprints will certainly show. And be very careful not to get any splinters or thorns in your feet."

"I still don't really believe this," said James, in a daze.

"So go out into the garden and just walk about. You'll soon find out," advised Brenda.

He hesitated, then opened the door and stepped outside cautiously. Immediately he turned back.

"How long is this going to last?" he

asked. It was important to know that, of course.

"It would be best if you came back inside and dressed in about half an hour," advised Brenda.

In the straggling, weed-ridden garden, it seemed strange to be wandering about like that. He could see nothing of himself whatever, but on the other hand ... what if Brenda had given him a drink of something which merely made him *think* he was invisible, while all the time ... ?

Then he realised that a couple of people were walking up the path towards him! He crouched down among the tall weeds at once, so they wouldn't be able to see him.

It was a man and a woman, both quite old, he could see as he peered through the weeds.

"This can't be the house," the man was saying irritably. "It's the wrong one entirely." Then they stopped on the path, undecided.

What he realised now was that he had never seen these two people before. They were complete strangers. So not only did he not know who they were, but that meant they wouldn't know who he was, either.

It was worth the risk, he decided. He came out from behind the weeds and started dancing about. If they looked in his direction they would be certain to see him – if he wasn't really invisible, that was.

Both the man and the woman glanced towards him with no expression of surprise at all. This was terrific! He really *was* invisible!

As well as delivering her paper, James visited Brenda each evening – except on Sundays, of course, when there was no evening paper and so no excuse to visit her and when it was raining, because of what she'd said about that.

She would never give him more than just about half a mugful of the strange brew, which she now kept in a special bottle on one of her shelves.

Brenda herself, though, would never touch it. He did try to persuade her once, but as she explained, she had to remain visible just in case anything ever went wrong and she had to prepare the antidote. It would be difficult if she couldn't see where her hands were to measure out the precise quantity of herbs. He could understand that.

While he was invisible he would wander round the streets, just for the fun of it, and afterwards return to Brenda's house in good time to get dressed before he reappeared.

"Never go near your own home or street, though, James," Brenda had told him. "Not while you're invisible."

"Why not?" he asked.

"You might accidentally step into a puddle or something and leave footprints which people might be able to identify. No-one else must know. This is our secret."

He had never had a secret before, so of course he did as she said. The trouble was that before long he was beginning to find the strange experience a little boring. He needed to do something more adventurous, something even more entertaining.

He thought about it. Then one Saturday afternoon, when the papers had arrived early, decided to ask.

"Brenda," he said tentatively.

"Yes, James?"

"Do you think you could make me invisible for, say, a couple of hours – now?"

Brenda considered, looking at him carefully. He didn't need to hurry home, because his parents were out and wouldn't miss him no matter what time he arrived back. He would like, he explained hopefully, to go into town, just to see what it was like to be invisible amongst a lot of people.

Brenda was a little doubtful.

"Then you'll have to be extra careful," she advised him. "Make sure you don't get your feet trodden on. But if you're sure ... All right. Then later I'll have a big surprise waiting for you."

"What's it going to be?" he asked

eagerly.

"Now if I told you, it wouldn't be a surprise, would it?"

She poured him a whole mug of the sweet, brown liquid and gave it to him. He was getting undressed even before he had vanished, because by now he was no longer embarrassed in the slightest because of the great secret between them. Then, when he had finally disappeared, he dashed off down the road.

It was great fun. In town he ran down the pavement, tripping people up – but not old people, of course – and opened and closed the doors of shops. He nipped inside a department store and ran round the counters stirring up everything which was laid out, running amongst the people who were watching the moving items in amazement.

Then, outside, he came across the woman who stood on the corner of one of the main roads every Saturday, selling flowers from a huge basket. He stood and watched her for a few seconds before deciding what to do. Then he bent over, picked the basket up, and with a quick heave threw it into the air.

At once a crowd gathered – as you would expect when an enormous flower basket suddenly rose into the air like that and then turned over, apparently all by itself!

James picked up a few of the fallen flowers and flung them up as well. The woman had hardly any left now anyway, and was not as if he was doing any real harm.

James laughed. It was so funny, but tried to suppress it in case anyone could tell exactly where the sound was coming from. A police car drew up and two policemen climbed out and walked briskly towards the flower-seller to find out the reason for all the fuss. That was when James decided it was time he left.

He would be quite all right, as the effect of what Brenda had given him to drink would not wear off for about another hour yet. That was plenty of time for him to return to her house and find out what the big surprise was going to be.

He turned, and began to saunter off through the crowd.

He was most surprised when one of the policemen took hold of him, but he didn't struggle. He would just wait for his chance to get away again. The policeman had obviously caught him by sheer accident, and sooner or later was bound to slacken his grip, then James would simply be able to slip away unseen.

He wondered how the policeman felt, having hold of nothing. He chuckled quietly to himself. He guessed that the policeman was as astonished to be holding an invisible bare arm as James himself was to be caught so accidentally.

But it wasn't like that!

"Come along, sonny," said the policeman, kindly. "You come with me into this nice, warm police car. I expect you find it a bit chilly like that, don't you? So you get into this car and make yourself warm, eh?"

*　　*　　*　　*　　*

"Well, whatever happened to him, then?" the customer was asking Mr Grimes, the newsagent.

"I can't understand it! He was such a nice lad, but you know that old house at the end of Moat Road, the one that's due for demolition? Well, it turns out he used to go there every night, take all his clothes off and then walk around the street, just like that. It's a wonder somebody didn't hit him. You'll never guess what was found inside that house."

"What?" asked the customer.

"Dozens of copies of the *Evening Mail*, all folded neatly in the middle of the rubble which used to be the kitchen floor. He'd been putting them there every night for months! The poor kid's in a mental home now, of course, No hope for him, I've been told. Thinks he's invisible, or something. It's his parents I feel sorry for."

*　　*　　*　　*　　*

Darren, the new newspaper lad for Grimes's,

had just delivered his final paper when he saw a movement at the back door of the last house along the road. That was odd, he thought. He'd heard it was going to be pulled down, yet now it had a new roof and window frames, and fresh curtains at the windows.

Then he saw somebody beckoning to him, so he opened the gate and walked up the path, which was rather overgrown with weeds. It was a woman standing there, so it seemed safe to approach her.

"Are you the newspaper lad?" she asked.

Darren nodded. She was quite young and very attractive.

"Well, I'd like the evening paper delivered, if you don't mind. Now, I don't want you to push it through the letterbox ..."

THE DISAPPEARANCE OF SAMANTHA

It was when Samantha was about eight years old that she made a very strange announcement.

"You know," she told her parents solemnly, "I don't think I'm really here at all."

"What an odd thing to say, Samantha!" exclaimed her mother.

"I've just decided it must be true," she replied.

Samantha had been adopted by Mr and Mrs Williams when she was just a few months old. As a tiny baby, she had been left on the doorstep of a hospital late one August night, with no explanation and nothing but the baby clothes she was dressed in at the time. There had just been a little note attached to her sleeve with a pink ribbon to say that her name was Samantha. It was never discovered who her real parents were.

Mr and Mrs Williams had no children of their own, but there were no problems with Samantha. For one thing, they made sure they didn't spoil their adopted daughter. What was more, they had made it quite clear to her, as soon as she was old enough to understand, that they were not her real parents.

What they did point out to her, though, was that of all the babies available, they had chosen *her*. She was very special to them.

Samantha grew up to be a perfectly ordinary little girl. Even when she was six and began to invent imaginary playmates for herself, Mr and Mrs Williams were not worried. Lots of children did that. It was not uncommon, just a phase which soon passed.

They were now, however, rather alarmed to hear what she was telling them about not really being there!

"What makes you think that?" her father asked, humouring her.

"Well," said Samantha carefully, "it's something I've found out. And it's got to mean that, either I'm not really here, or I am here but nobody else is!"

If her father was worried, he tried not to show it.

"I don't think that makes much

sense," he said, smiling.

"No, I don't suppose it does, really." Then Samantha paused for a moment, frowning. "I can walk through things," she added casually. "That's what makes me certain."

"Really? What sort of things?" asked her father, amused now.

"Walls," said Samantha. "I can walk straight through them. So if I can do that, then they can't really exist, can they? Or if the walls are there, then I'm not. Don't you think?" she smiled sweetly at them.

Mrs Williams was not impressed.

"You know you shouldn't make up stories like that," she said firmly.

"It's just another phase she's going through," said Mr Williams wisely after Sam had gone out to play in the large front garden of their house. "I'll go and have a little talk with her, and put her right."

He walked into the garden after her.

"I think you're old enough now to know the difference between what's real and what's made-up, Sam," he said.

She looked up from one of her dolls. This one was being troublesome because it was warm outside, so she was taking off its clothes.

"I know that," she said, smiling even more sweetly. "But I know that one of us is real, and one of us isn't. The only thing I'm not sure about, is which. It's when I found myself walking through a brick wall the other day that I found out about it."

"Yes. Of course," said Mr Williams, nodding, as if walking through a brick wall was the most natural thing anyone could do. "Now you just show me how you do it. Walk through the wall of the house," he suggested, pointing.

"That wouldn't be any good," objected Samantha. "It doesn't work if anyone's watching."

She was making this up as she went along, of course, Mr Williams could tell. He crouched down on the lawn at the side of her.

"So when did you find you could do this?" he persisted. He was quite amused, really.

"We've got the builders in at school," said Samantha, without a moment's thought. She really was a bright little girl. "They'd blocked off the path in front of the school. You know we line up in the yard at the back? Well, two days ago – Thursday, it was – I was late, so instead of going all the way round, I just walked through the school instead."

Of course she was telling the truth now, he knew that. Except that what she had actually done was to walk into the school through a door, go along the corridors into the yard and through another door at the back. That's how she had really walked through the school.

Samantha looked surprised.

"It wasn't like that. I walked through the nearest wall, then through the walls of all the classrooms, then out through the back wall when no one was looking," she said earnestly. "It was the quickest way, you see. I didn't want the teachers to know I was late."

Mr Williams was no longer amused.

"So why don't you walk through walls all the time, then?" he asked, trying to sound reasonable.

Samantha looked even more surprised.

"That would look silly," she replied.

She'd always had a vivid imagination, he considered, as he strolled back indoors, leaving her to look after her doll which had been complaining about the heat.

As soon as he entered the house, he saw her coming towards him from the kitchen with a glass of lemonade in her hand. That gave him a real start! He had only just left her in the front garden – yet here she was coming from the kitchen at the *back* of their house!

There was only one explanation. She must have run like mad round the house as soon as he had gone, run in through the back door, poured herself the lemonade, and was now walking calmly towards him.

Unless ... no that was just not possible! The really worrying part, though, was that

Samantha was not in the least out of breath.

"How did you get there?" he demanded.

"I walked in through the dining room wall," she said, "like I told you I could."

Then she went out again through the open front door, as if nothing had happened.

"It's not like the time when she invented other children to play with," Mr Williams explained to his wife a few moments later. "She knew they were imaginary, but now – well, she's doing everything she can to convince us. I can't make this out at all."

But suppose, he thought suddenly, their daughter really did believe she could walk through solid objects? What if she wasn't trying to convince them that it was true, but trying to convince herself instead? That could be serious.

"You think she's deranged, then? That's rubbish!" retorted Mrs Williams, who was watering some indoor plants at the time. The pots stood on a table in the window. "I'll show you." She opened the window and called. "Samantha! I want you for a minute."

Samantha came running. She entered through the front door and came into the room.

"Could you go upstairs and fetch me a clean hankie from my drawer?" her mother asked.

As Samantha turned to go out of the

room again, Mrs Williams said,

"If you want your father and me to believe this nonsense, why don't you go straight up through the ceiling?"

"I couldn't do that," said Samantha seriously. "You'd be watching, and anyway, I can't float, you know."

Then she left, and they heard her clumping up the stairs on her errand.

That settled it. For all they knew, one of these days she might decide she could float after all, and try jumping from a bedroom window. They couldn't risk that.

On Monday, Mr Williams made an appointment to see the doctor who had known Samantha since she'd been a baby. But he did not let Samantha know where he was going.

The doctor was brisk and reassuring.

"It's a harmless fantasy," she said. "See if you can think of some little task to set her which can only be done by walking through a wall. When she finds out for herself that she really can't, she'll know she's just been playing a game and you'll hear no more about it."

The doctor wasn't a lot of help, Mr Williams thought gloomily as he left the surgery, but an idea soon came to him.

It was the following weekend when he happened to notice that Samantha had come in because it had started to rain. She had accidentally left one of her dolls out in the garden. She had carted the rest of them upstairs, where she was no doubt tucking them in, or something.

He drew his wife's attention to the doll through the window of the front room downstairs.

"Now we'll cure her," he chuckled. "We'll tell her to go out and bring that old doll inside. As soon as she's outside, we'll lock all the doors so she can't come back in again unless we open them for her. That'll put her right."

Mrs Williams nodded approvingly.

"Bound to work," she said.

She went to the stairs and called.

"You've left one of your dolls out in the rain. Better fetch it in before it gets soaked."

At once Samantha scampered down the stairs, opened the front door and ran out to collect it. Mr Williams promptly shut it behind her while Mrs Williams hurried to lock the back door as well. Then they waited in the front room.

They heard her try the front door, then patter round the side of the house. Then they heard the kitchen door rattle. Then there was silence.

The next thing they heard was Samantha going back upstairs!

When they dashed out of the room,

she was sitting on the stairs with the wet doll in her hands, wiping it dry with her hankie.

"I've got her," she said, unconcerned.

They followed her into her room. Mrs Williams sat on the bed. Suddenly she felt weak at the knees. Mr Williams stared at Samantha and the doll in disbelief.

"How did ... how did you get back into the house?" he asked, trying to keep his voice calm.

"I found the doors were locked, so I came in through the kitchen wall," she replied. "I squeezed through the space next to the refrigerator."

"Now this has gone far enough," said her mother, rather crossly.

Mr Williams shot back down the stairs. When he returned he was looking shaken. The doors were still locked, sure enough, and no windows had been left open, either.

"I just don't understand this," he said, and sat on the bed as well. "There just has to be some proper explanation. And we're all staying here in your room until we find what it is!"

"It's like I told you," remarked Samantha. "I'm not really here at all. Either that, or nothing else is."

"Let's – let's think about this," said Mr Williams, still bewildered. "If we're not here with you, but you are here all by yourself ...

then where are your mother and me, if we're not really here at all?"

"Perhaps it means I just imagine you," said Samantha after a moment's thought. "Perhaps I imagine everything. Like you, this house, school, everything. Perhaps there's just me."

There was silence.

"Of course, it could be the other way round," she added cheerfully. "Perhaps you're here, but you just imagine me."

She didn't seem to be bothered in the slightest. Mrs Williams wasn't sure she understood any of this. She was certain that at that moment she was sitting on Samantha's bed though. That felt real – right at this moment. Mr Williams had much the same thoughts.

"I wouldn't be surprised if one of us disappeared soon, you know," remarked Samantha.

"And go where?" asked Mr Williams sharply.

Samantha shook her head.

"I don't know. I just think it could happen, that's all."

They gave up. Before long, it had stopped raining. It had been quite a downpour while it had lasted. Now Samantha wheeled her doll's pram out into the front garden, carefully placed her entire collection of dolls in it and covered them up.

Mr and Mrs Williams watched anxiously from the window.

"I can guess what she's thinking of doing now," said Mrs Williams, thoroughly recovered and ready to stand no more nonsense. "If she heads for the gate, I'm going straight out there to stop her and bring her back. I'm not allowing her to walk off up the road and then pretend she's disappeared."

Samantha began to wheel the doll's pram across the lawn ... not towards the gate, but instead towards the shrubbery at the end of the garden. She'd come to no harm there, even if she tried to hide in it, because there was a wall the other side.

"I still don't understand how she managed to fetch that doll in from the rain, though," muttered Mr Williams.

"We'll find out before long," replied Mrs Williams grimly.

They watched Samantha for a few minutes as she trundled the pram round the lawn. She was only playing at taking the dolls for a walk, so it was safe to leave her.

The telephone rang. It was Mrs Williams's sister. They both spoke to her.

A few minutes later they returned to look through the window to see what Samantha was doing now. She was nowhere to be seen. Both of them dashed outside.

"Now calm down," said Mr Williams,

very quietly. "I know where she is. Just as I said. Look."

On the grass, where it had been made wet by the rain, the tracks of the pram wheels were clearly marked. First they went round and round the lawn, overlapping each other, then they headed towards the shrubbery. There were no tracks returning.

"As I thought, she's hiding in the shrubbery," said Mr Williams. "Come on out now, Sam," he called. "You've had your fun."

Mrs Williams suddenly gave a little scream. At first her husband couldn't see what she was making a fuss about, until he saw where she was pointing.

They were very proud of the sundial. It stood on a little stone pedestal at the edge of the bushes which formed the shrubbery, where the sun could shine on it for most of the day. It gave their front garden that extra little touch, they thought.

"But look!" screamed Mrs Williams.

The wheel tracks led straight towards the sundial. These were still visible on the grass on the other side of it.

But worst of all, they ran in a continuous, unbroken line on either side of the little stone pedestal, as if Samantha had not even noticed that the sundial was there at all and had wheeled her doll's pram right through it ...

THE EVERLASTING DAY

It was going to be another hot day, thought John as he was woken by the sunlight already dappling the roof of the little two-man tent he shared with Richard.

This was a really good summer Scout camp – the best he could remember. It had never rained and the sun shone all day long. It was simply brilliant! He was glad he had come.

John looked at his wrist watch, untied the flaps of the tent and ran along to the other three tents in his pyjamas. He bashed on the canvas sides with the flat of his hand.

"Come on, get up!" he called. "Don't let the sun scorch your eyes out." His mother often said that if he was late up.

There was a vague stirring inside each tent. Steve's head poked out through the flaps of one of them.

"Morning, John," he said sleepily, and went back inside again. He always did that first thing in the morning.

Then, having woken the others, John went back to his own tent. Richard had already gathered his towel and soap and was now fiddling around in his rucksack to find his toothbrush and toothpaste.

It's always like that, John thought to himself. Every morning, without fail, Richard never seemed to be able to find his toothbrush at the same time as he found his soap and towel.

John dressed quickly, leaving off his shirt, then snatched the things he needed and ran with them to the washbasins at the far end of the field. They had made them themselves out of metal bowls held up on long sticks lashed together. Richard was hurrying along behind as he always did.

They weren't the first to arrive – they never were. The Peewit patrol were invariably there first. Then some of the Raven patrol would stroll up. The Curlew patrol weren't there at all, because they'd washed earlier. That was because they were on cooks' duty that morning, preparing breakfast over the fire – porridge, followed by bacon and eggs, and tea. The porridge and the tea were already steaming. Wood smoke rose lazily and happily from the kitchen area.

John liked being at the annual Scout camp because it was fun, exciting and adventurous. He was the patrol leader of the Owls, and Richard was his second.

The one thing he had not been able to solve was how to get all his patrol up in the morning. Apart from himself and Richard, the others were always last at the washing area. When he'd finished having his own wash, he'd go and roust them out.

They were just emerging by the time he got back.

"Get a move on, you lot," he called. "We'll be last to breakfast again."

"We always are," said Steve.

That was true as well. They were the last to breakfast every morning. Strange. Come to think of it, he couldn't remember when it had been otherwise.

After breakfast was over and the washing-up had been done, they had to get themselves properly dressed with their kit laid neatly outside the tents on their ground-sheets, and not a speck of litter to be seen anywhere in their patrol area. Inspection was at half-past nine.

They managed to line up just in time, with John as the patrol leader at one end, and Richard as the second-in-command at the other, with the rest of the patrol in between the two of them.

They were now all in full Scout

uniform and standing smartly to attention when the Scoutmaster and his assistant came round. The Scoutmaster carried a notebook in which he awarded points as each patrol won them.

John gave the Scout salute, as he was supposed to, and the Scoutmaster saluted back. Then he walked along the line, inspecting both them and their kit. At the same time the Assistant Scoutmaster, Jim Smithers, was poking his head inside each tent in turn and then coming out again.

"Find anything?" asked the Scoutmaster.

"As usual, absolutely perfect," said Jim, smiling. "Not a scrap of litter anywhere."

"Full points, then," said the Scoutmaster, and they moved on to inspect the Ravens.

There'd always be two scraps of torn paper found there, John knew, with a point deducted for each. They were there every morning. You'd think they'd learn.

In the meantime the Owl patrol dragged their kit back inside the tents. The morning inspection was over.

A whistle blew – twice. That meant that only the patrol leaders were wanted. A whole series of blasts on the whistle would have meant everybody. John ran over to join the other three patrol leaders at the

Scoutmaster's tent.

Funny, he thought, that whistle always went at the precise moment before he'd stuffed all his kit back into his rucksack, and he always had a pair of socks left out.

They were reminded what the activity was for that morning. Each patrol had to devise and erect a bridge made only of wood, rope and string, in different parts of the field. Then to prove that they had made it properly, the whole patrol had to walk across it, one at a time, without it collapsing.

John knew exactly how he was going to get his patrol to do that. First they'd use string to lash together thick pieces of wood to make two cross-shaped frames for each end. Then they'd stretch a rope between them for walking on and fasten other ropes on either side to act as handrails. Then they'd tie more ropes to the frames at each end which would be attached to tent pegs driven firmly into the ground to hold the whole thing up.

It would take all morning to construct. Richard was bound to fall off halfway across when he volunteered to test it first, because he was clumsy. But it would work, all right. It always did. They could easily have crossed a real stream safely over that bridge, or even a ravine.

Then it was dinner time. They always ate sitting on the grass, with the plate on their knees. He sat with Steve, the latest recruit to his patrol.

"I think this is great," declared Steve happily. "I'll always remember the day we built a bridge, you know. 17th July, 1943. And do you realise," he added, "that it'll never be 17th July, 1943, ever again?"

"Well, of course it won't," said John. "It couldn't be, could it?"

"I wonder if in ten year's time I'll still remember today, though. Do you think the war will be over by then? It'd be terrible if it was still going on."

"Of course it will," said John confidently. "It'll be over by next year at the latest. Bound to be."

He certainly hoped so. He hadn't seen his dad for three years. He was somewhere in North Africa, but he wasn't sure where because he wasn't allowed to say in his letters.

There was to be a wide game that evening, with half of the Scout troop against the other half, while the Scoutmaster and Jim acted as umpires. The Owls were to join with the Ravens to attack, while the Peewits and the Curlews were to defend the camp first.

Each attacker was given three pieces of paper with his name on, each representing one "life". The object was for the attackers to get into the camp without being captured by the other side.

Each time they were caught, they had

to hand over one life, then go back a hundred paces and wait one minute before they could move again. Lose all three lives, and they were out of the game and had to return to camp. Then after an hour it would all be reversed, and the winners would be the side with most lives intact. It was rough and tumble, of course, but great fun, especially stalking through the undergrowth without being seen. No one got hurt, apart from the odd bruise, even when they were jumped on.

It was at the very end of the game with everyone back in camp and gathered round the camp fire totting up the scores to decide the winners, when suddenly a heavy droning sound was heard, coming from the direction of the trees at the edge of the field.

"It's a German bomber!" shouted the Scoutmaster in surprise, and they all scattered and lay flat as the aircraft, with large black crosses marked on its sides, flew low overhead.

Bombers shouldn't be flying round here. This was a peaceful part of the country, miles from any wartime risk, which was why it had been chosen for the summer camp. This one must have got lost.

They heard a tremendous, loud crump! and there was a sudden bright flash as a single bomb fell and exploded.

"I don't think it could have done much damage," remarked the Scoutmaster thoughtfully, as they all picked themselves up again. "Getting rid of its last bomb, I expect. It must have dropped in the open field the other side of the village. Okay, excitement over. We were lucky there was only one. Time for bed. Lights out in about half an hour."

The totally unexpected danger was over almost as soon as it had begun, but there was much excited chatter, as they headed back to their tents.

"That's another thing I'll remember today for as well," announced Steve with satisfaction. "Something I'll be able to tell 'em when I get home. Not that I expect they'll believe me."

"Well, they should. After all, it is wartime," said Richard.

"Not out here it isn't," said Steve firmly. "Who'd have expected a bomber to get lost over a little village called St Marychurch? I bet it's not even marked on their maps."

That was when John began to feel strangely uneasy. He couldn't quite put a finger on what was wrong exactly. It was something to do with Steve and what he had said, not only just now, but at some time previously that day.

Somehow it had something to do with the date, though he couldn't think of anything special about that, not yet, anyway.

Perhaps it would come to him later.

Richard was about to fasten their tent flaps once they were inside, but before he did he poked his head out and looked at the sky.

"It's a beautiful clear night," he said. "Stars out all over the place."

John crouched down and looked with him. Their little two-man tent wasn't big enough for either of them to stand upright inside.

"There's the Great Bear," he said, pointing. "So – " he followed the line of the last two stars – "there's the north star over there."

Another useful thing he'd learned in the Scouts, he decided, was being able to tell the compass direction from the stars. It was always the same routine, every night before they went to sleep, to look at the stars. Somehow it was satisfying, even though he was pretty sure that Richard managed to say the same thing each time they did.

Then they got into their sleeping bags, lay down and both fell asleep almost at once.

The morning dawned sunny and it was soon hot. John wasn't surprised. He was sure it was all going to be great fun again. He wouldn't mind staying here, with his friends, for the rest of his life. No more school, no more nagging big sister to bother him, just hot, sunny, never-ending exciting days.

Impossible, of course. Nothing could

ever remain the same for ever. He'd have to grow up, nothing could prevent that. The Scout camp would have to come to an end within a week. Then it would all be back to normal. Sooner or later the war would be over and all this would just be a memory of really happy times.

No one later, who hadn't been around at the time, would ever believe that life during wartime could have been happy, he pondered. They would imagine it was all bombs and air-raid shelters. For some people who lived in the big cities, it was. He'd read about it in the papers and heard it on the news. For him and the rest of them there, however, apart from last night's totally unexpected incident, it was a happy time.

The day's activities followed their usual course. Steve had made the same sort of comment about the date at dinnertime, but had obviously got it wrong this time since it was obviously now a day later, though John hadn't bothered to correct him.

Now it was the wide game again, with John's patrol and the Ravens on the attack. He happened to be by himself, and could hear the shouts of the defenders as they pounced on somebody not far away.

He crouched low, out of sight. He could tell from the voices that they'd got Richard again.

"Go on, you're supposed to hand a

life over," he heard Charles say. He was the Peewit patrol leader.

"You'll have to search me first," he heard Richard reply, as he always told them when he got caught. "I'm not handing a life over, just like that. There's no rule that says so."

"Turn him upside down and shake him," he heard, "see if it falls out."

"Ow!" That was Richard again. "You're still not having it if you can't find it."

"Then we'll undress you until we do," said Charles firmly. "Get his shorts off!"

John chuckled, and moved silently away. He knew that Richard always tucked his three pieces of paper inside his underpants. They never thought of searching there.

John decided to do something different for once, something he had never done before. He wouldn't head towards the camp, hoping to avoid the defenders, as he usually did. He'd skirt round the back of them instead. He had plenty of time. He found a hedge, and slipped through a hole in it on to a narrow lane.

He wasn't sure where he was now, but if he kept in the general direction of the camp to his right, he'd be near the entrance to their field before long. The defenders would never expect him to come from that direction.

The lane was longer than he had

expected and didn't seem to be going in the right direction. He ran on, only to find a church in front of him. He'd reached the village.

None of them had been there before. They had been instructed not to go there, for some reason which hadn't been explained, but there would be free time the following afternoon when they could, the Scoutmaster had said.

Still, he couldn't help that now. He was already there.

He remembered that when they had arrived in the coach he had seen this church not far behind the cross-roads where they had turned left for the field where they were camping. So if he walked to the other side of it, he'd find those cross-roads then be back in camp in a matter of minutes with all his lives intact. This was really going to surprise them!

Then he paused. He could feel, strangely, yet again that there was something slightly wrong about this, a sense that things were not quite as they should be. It was almost as if this was something he should not be doing, something forbidden.

He glanced casually up at the wall of the church and found a stone plaque fixed to it. He was about to go on when he happened to notice a name on it, among many others, which seemed familiar: *Richard Hughes*. That was the same as Richard's. Strange! Though of course it was hardly an unusual name.

When he looked over the rest he found there was a Steven Chalmers, and a Charles Ingram, and a Jim ... In bewilderment, he read the rest of the list inscribed on the plaque. They were the names of all his friends in camp, every single one of them – and much, much worse, he could see his own name among them!

With growing horror now, he looked up to read the words at the top:

In sad memory of the members of the 6th Devisham Scout Troop, killed by a bomb ...

And at the foot was a date: 17th July, 1943.

He turned in panic, and ran back the way he had come. He had to tell the Scoutmaster about this. This couldn't be true. There was no way it could be – could it?

He found the same hole in the hedge, scrambled through, and returned panting to where he had last been.

He could still hear Richard complaining as they searched him for one of his lives.

He knew what to do now. If he headed towards that clump of bushes, and kept low, he'd avoid the three he knew always lay in wait on the other side of it and get into camp totally unchallenged. It always worked.

There was something he kept trying to remember as he passed silently by, but he wasn't sure what it was. He just couldn't recall it at all. It was something very recent, something to do with a date, and some names. No doubt he'd think of it later.

They were gathered round the camp fire again and the Scoutmaster was totting up the scores from the lives which had been handed in, when suddenly there was a heavy droning sound from over the trees at the far end of the field.

"It's a German bomber!" shouted the Scoutmaster.

THE GHOST OF HARRY

It wasn't too bad being a ghost, Harry decided, once he'd got used to the idea. Better than when he'd lived in a children's home, anyway. Too many rules and regulations there. They'd tried putting him into a foster home, but that hadn't worked out.

"Too boisterous," they said. "And he keeps tormenting the dog."

The next foster home had been no better. A really boring middle-aged couple, the sort who seemed to have been born middle-aged, no fun at all. Do this, do that, all the time.

In a way, it was their fault he'd turned into a ghost. That fatal day he'd collected his belongings, stuffed them into a suitcase, and hurried out of the house when they weren't looking and, because he was in such a hurry to get back to the children's home, hadn't noticed the car.

So now what? He had expected when he became a ghost there'd be lots of other ghosts around as well, thousands of them probably. After all, where else did dead people go?

As it was – nothing. No other ghosts at all. He was the only ghost in town, as far as he could tell.

Of course he could still see people. The only real difference was, they couldn't see him. He could still walk along the pavements, see grass and trees and all that – and, he was delighted to discover, could actually walk through things.

He'd discovered this interesting little trick by accident. He was wandering along the pavement, pondering that he never needed to eat, which was a pity, because some food he had really liked, and never needed to sleep either, which he didn't mind at all – and he had decided to cross over the road to look in a shop window. Even if he couldn't eat sweets and chocolates any more, at least he could still look at them!

Just as he'd reached the far side, a gang of youths came hurtling towards him, bunched up in a tight group. So, without thinking, he moved quickly out of their way, to find that he'd gone clean through the wall of the shop and was now inside!

That had been an interesting surprise. He practised walking through the same shop wall a few times, then jumping through it and back again. The shop windows were just as good, with not even a crack in them afterwards to show that he'd just gone through. Good fun, really.

But, what was a ghost supposed to *do*? He didn't see any sense in being one at all. It might have been different if he'd had any grieving relatives who couldn't see him any more. He didn't think he would have liked that, being unable to comfort them, unable to tell them it was all right, not to worry, it hadn't hurt at all.

That was another thing – it hadn't hurt in the slightest when it happened. When the car had hit him and flung him across the street, he'd just had time to say "Da –"

And by the time he'd reached "-mn!" there he was, a ghost!

He thought he knew why it hadn't hurt. He remembered another boy at the children's home who had had an accident, when he'd been hit by a brick and knocked unconscious. Later on, he told Harry that he couldn't remember a thing about it. He could remember the start of the accident, when he'd seen the brick coming and tried to dodge it. Also, he could recall lying in a hospital bed, but in between – nothing whatsoever. It was, he decided, the convenient way things were – when something nasty happens to you, you actually know nothing about it afterwards.

He decided to return for a visit to the children's home where he found some of them playing football. Harry wanted to join in, but there was not a thing he could do. His foot passed clean through the ball every time!

He couldn't even be the referee, because when he tried to snatch the whistle from Mr Woolley, his hand passed through that as well. All he could do was watch. That, frankly, was annoying.

Okay, ghosts were supposed to wander at night rattling chains and making eerie noises to frighten people, weren't they? And he knew where there were some chains. Some old rusty ones were kept in a shed round the back. He went to find them.

Waste of time! When he reached down to pick them up, he couldn't. Like the football, and the referee's whistle and walls for that matter, his hand simply went right through them!

Anyway, he decided to have a go without the chains. He hung around until it was bedtime, and dark, and then slipped upstairs to the room where Fred and George slept. He stood by the window and went "Hoo-hoo!" mournfully and eerily.

Fred and George were not asleep, but

talking to each other. It seemed they couldn't see or hear him at all.

"Shame about Harry," Fred was saying. "He always was a laugh. Pain in the bum, but a laugh all the same."

Pain in the bum? Harry was outraged! So that's what Fred had thought about him, was it? If he'd known, he wouldn't have given him half of that bar of chocolate he'd nicked from a shop once. He'd have eaten the lot himself.

"Yeah, pain in the bum. You're right about that." That was George.

Harry moaned more loudly, just to scare them, and when that didn't work, tried dragging the bedclothes off each of the beds instead. Complete failure again.

He stomped off to see if he could scare a few of the girls. Sally and Rosina, they'd do. Rosina always scared easily, while Sally was one of those who thought she knew it all.

In their room, at the other side of the children's home, where all the girls slept, he tried again. Still nothing, even though he could tell that neither of them were asleep yet.

He concentrated hard, and suddenly ...

Rosina stared into the darkness, and screamed.

Then Sally sat up in her bed, stared as well, and exclaimed,

"Why, it's Harry!"

She didn't seem scared in the slightest. Rather disappointing, actually.

"Shut up, Rosina," she said briskly. "So you're a ghost now, are you? Can you speak to us, then?"

"No," said Harry, rather put out.

"You just did," retorted Sally. "Shut up, Rosina," she said again, "or someone'll hear us. Well," she resumed, regarding Harry thoughtfully, "what's it like?"

"Boring," said Harry, truthfully. "I can pass through things, and all that, but that's all. Not at all like what I expected. Aren't you scared I'm here?"

"No," said Sally bluntly.

"Nor me," quavered Rosina.

"Yes, you are," said Harry. "I can tell you are."

"You shouldn't be here," said Rosina, plucking up a little more courage now. "You should only be haunting the boys' bedrooms. This isn't right," she added primly.

"Got any friends with you?" Sally suddenly asked, rather too eagerly.

"No. Why, should I have?"

"Just a thought," replied Sally, rather dreamily. "I was just thinking, if you had, we might be able to have a party."

Suddenly the room was full of ghosts, appearing out of nowhere! Harry was very surprised.

"Verily, a party?" said one. He was

wearing such old-fashioned clothes that Harry wondered how long it was since he'd been around in real life. It must have been an extremely long time ago. "Obediah," he introduced himself. "I was overrun, with fatal results, by a carriage when I was fourteen."

"Where have you all been?" demanded Harry. "I've been around for ages and haven't seen any of you before, yet now you all turn up – just like that."

"The chance of a party's different," sniffed another ghost, who seemed to have emerged from the wardrobe.

Harry looked around. All boy ghosts, like himself, he noticed. Sally was getting out of bed now, shamelessly, in her nightie.

"Well, as long as we're quiet I don't suppose it'll matter," she announced, and put her cassette player on at low volume.

But it was not low enough! Before long, the door suddenly opened and half a dozen more girls came into the room.

"We thought so. It sounded like a party!" exclaimed one of them. That was Janet, a tall girl Harry hadn't liked very much in his previous existence, but to his surprise, she began to dance with him.

A few minutes later, the party was in full swing. Even the more timid girls were dancing with the ghosts, some of whom had to be taught how to, as they hadn't been around for a considerable number of years.

Eventually a church clock struck somewhere outside the building. Harry didn't hear it, but all the other ghosts did. The one in the strange clothes tapped him on the shoulder.

"'Tis midnight," announced Obediah.

"So?" said Harry, who was enjoying himself at the time. When he looked around and saw that the other ghostly visitors were standing quite still, he stopped as well.

"Time we left," announced Obediah, and began to fade, while the one who had emerged from the wardrobe now began to dissolve.

"See you tomorrow, gentle ladies," said Obediah faintly just before he disappeared completely.

"Gentle ladies? Cor!" giggled Rosina. She'd changed considerably for the better since he'd first appeared, decided Harry with interest.

Then the room was empty apart from the girls, and Harry.

"Better be going myself, then," he said.

Almost before he knew it, he'd vanished. He knew that he'd vanished because he could see the girls looking around trying to find him.

The trouble was, the other ghosts had disappeared so completely that he could no longer see them.

He shrugged and wandered off. Not much else he could do, really, in the circumstances. He did wonder where all the others had really gone, but decided that, like himself, they just hung around hopefully.

The following night Harry turned up early, timing it so he'd be there just as the girls were supposed to have gone to bed. He knew when that would be, because it was a fixed time for all of them in the children's home. He waited by the church until the clock struck the appropriate time, then walked across, through the wall of the building, concentrated hard, and materialised.

Everyone else must have had the same idea, because they all arrived more or less together. Somebody had even managed to get a few cans of pop in – no use to the boys, of course, but the girls liked it.

Before long, some of the girls were pairing off with a ghost of their choice. What's more, the boys seemed to enjoy it hugely. Harry had a kiss with Sally and found that he liked it as well. It hadn't been like this when he'd been alive, he thought.

The news soon spread, at first with disbelief, then with annoyance, among the boys in the home.

"Those girls," said Fred angrily to George several evenings later, "don't take any notice of us boys any more. It's not right."

"Partying every night, they are," agreed George – "and until midnight."

"We should tell Mr Woolley," said Fred, glumly.

"Now who'd believe us?" asked George. "No, this has to be something we sort out ourselves, before Mr Woolley and the other staff even find out. Tell you what," he added, "all of us boys – real boys, that is – need to get something organised!"

"It's all Harry's fault," said Fred, darkly. "I overheard that he's always there. You know, I thought I saw him in our room one night, but didn't like to mention it, not knowing what he might be up to."

"He hasn't changed then," remarked George. "Still a pain in the bum, like he always was."

They called a meeting, round the back of the building near where they played football, where none of the staff would be likely to see them.

"What we've got to do," declared Fred, "is get all those ghosts away from here, once and for all. I mean, they're getting so noisy I can't get to sleep – not until midnight, anyway."

"The staff'll start to hear them soon," agreed another of the boys.

"Haven't had a proper night's sleep

for nearly a week," complained another boy.

"The only thing to do," said George slowly, "is find some way of persuading them to go away. I vote one or two of us go along tonight, find out what's what, then work something out from there."

"Those girls won't let us in," said Fred. "I tried the other night, and Sally threw me out."

"They couldn't if several of us went," suggested George thoughtfully.

So that's what they did. Fred and George were nominated. That night the two of them crept cautiously and quietly, so the staff wouldn't hear them, across to the girls' rooms. When they burst in they found the party was well under way.

"Greetings," said Obediah, seeing them first, "and to be sure you are welcome, verily." For the moment Obediah seemed to be taking a rest from his exertions, and was willing to chat ...

"Run down by a carriage, you say?" asked Fred suddenly, with a glint in his eye. "So what happened to the driver?"

"'Twas Lord Millichamp's coachman, who fell off in the impact and himself ceased to exist," said Obediah. "The coach, too, was wrecked and never driven again in life."

"You mean –"

"Both are still around, usually past the church at midnight. I hear that folk do say the

121

coachman is headless, but that is without doubt nonsense. I speak regularly to him, and his head is invariably in its correct position."

"What are you two doing here?" demanded Sally loudly, having just disentangled herself from a passionate embrace with Harry, who was looking almost embarrassed.

"Just got an idea," replied Fred with a grin. "I'll tell you all about it in a minute."

He turned back to Obediah.

"Is it possible," he asked very cautiously, "for the coach to be summoned to the door, at midnight, say?"

"Assuredly. The coachman, one Wilkins, is of a friendly disposition."

"And it is – er – a large coach?" he asked casually. "Big enough, say, for this lot?" he asked, nodding around the room.

"Verily," replied Obediah. "Lord Millichamp did not stint on luxury. It was uncommonly large."

"Then how about –" began Fred, and whispered his plan to the now attentive Obediah, who shortly slipped away without anyone else noticing ...

"As long as you left quietly, nobody would know, would they, at least until it was too late?" explained Fred enthusiastically to his audience, who were now listening with great interest and, certainly among the girls, with a considerable amount of excitement.

The coach was already waiting outside the door as they left the building, with the coachman seated on his box at the front, his whip in his hand, and the ghosts of six impatient white horses below him.

Obediah bowed to each girl as she entered, each now wearing her outdoor clothes, then followed them into the coach. Then the other boy ghosts stepped in behind them. It got so full that some of them had to climb on top, where they sat grinning. Just before the coach moved off, Harry leaned out the window.

"Brilliant idea!" he said in admiration. "A real laugh. Though I didn't like what I heard you call me the other night, Fred."

Fred blushed.

"No hard feelings, though," said Harry, trying to shake his hand but somehow failing now. Perhaps it was because the church clock was already on the last stroke of midnight.

The ghostly horseman cracked his whip, the ghostly white horses strained, and the ghostly coach began to draw away. Fred and George could hear the excited chatter from the girls inside slowly becoming fainter, almost as if the volume was being turned down, then resolving into silence as the coach itself began to fade and the road began to show through where it had once been.

"So that's that," said George with satisfaction, and they crept back to their room and went to bed.

It caused a tremendous fuss, of course. Police were out for days trying to find who had abducted so many of the girls from the children's home, but failed to come up with any explanation at all. The newspapers were full of reports of false sightings for weeks afterwards until the interest died down.

It was now a lot more peaceful for the boys who lived in the children's home. In fact, a considerable relief. Added to which, the girls who eventually arrived to replace those who'd mysteriously disappeared, weren't such a nuisance as the previous lot.

So all in all, everyone was satisfied.

Other titles available in the *SCARUMS* series ...

	ISBN	COVER PRICE
Noises In The Night	1 84161 031 3	£2.99
The Ghost Train	1 84161 032 1	£2.99
The Werewolf Mask	1 84161 033 X	£2.99

Available from all good bookshops, or direct from the publisher. Please send a cheque or postal order for the cover price of the book/s, made payable to 'Ravette Publishing Ltd' and allow the following for postage and packing ...

UK & BFPO	50p for the first book & 30p per book thereafter
Europe & Eire	£1.00 for the first book & 50p per book thereafter
rest of the world	£1.80 for the first book & 80p per book thereafter

RAVETTE PUBLISHING LTD
Unit 3, Tristar Centre, Star Road, Partridge Green,
West Sussex RH13 8RA